LOSING *Manhattan*

A NAKED IN NEW YORK NOVEL

PEYTON JAMES

DEDICATION

To my family, who stood behind me and cheered me on.
To my dad, for his unwavering (and sometimes over-the-top) enthusiasm.
To my writing peeps, for their encouragement and imparted wisdom.
And for you, too. :+)

Thank you for reading!

CHAPTER *one*

In the four years since I moved to New York City, I've never dared to shop at the stores that line Fifth Avenue. Not just because I'm broke, but because my body isn't built to fit these high-end clothes.

I have curves—tits and ass as they say—and I'm damn proud of them. Or at least I was until today. Today, they're not working in my favor.

Inside the spacious dressing room at Sloane's on Fifth, I hook another set of hangers on the back of the door and toss my purse onto the fancy fabric bench. "None of this is going to fit, Tessa," I grumble. "Can we just go? This is embarrassing." Stripping a ruby-red sheath dress from its hanger, I hold it up to my chest and eye myself in the mirror before shaking my head. Nope. Not a chance. What the hell was Tessa thinking? I can't go to work looking like Jessica Rabbit! I toss the dress onto the bench and grab the teal bra that *I* picked out.

"If you want people to take you seriously, you have to look the part," she says. "This is Manhattan, Hannah. The *big leagues*. Trust me, okay?"

I sigh. She's right. It's going to hurt my wallet, but I'm desperate for nice clothes. As of this morning, I'm the newest graphic designer at Evans, Roth and Sloane, one of the largest corporations in North America. From restaurants to clothing lines, they do it all. There's no corner of any market they haven't touched. If this job works out, the ads I design will be plastered all over New York City. Hell, maybe all over the world.

"It's only a three-month contract," I say, fastening the lacy teal bra behind my back. "But it could lead to more. It *needs* to lead to more." Not even a Master's Degree is a guarantee of a good job these days. I need to do whatever it takes to make this permanent and work my way up the corporate ladder.

"It fits! And it's pretty," I say, moving closer to the mirror to admire the lace. Kinda sorta sexy, even on me.

"I told you. Here, try this, too." Tessa hands me a skirt and blouse over the door. "We'll have you looking like a bona fide Manhattanite in no time."

A girl can dream. Tessa didn't see the women who interviewed me. All of them prim and proper in tight pencil skirts and the latest designer shoes. Even the receptionist was better dressed than me. If I want to impress Sloane's team, I need to look like I belong. And if that means dropping a size or two to squeeze into his overpriced clothing line, then dammit, I'll do it. I need all the brownie points I can get. If this job doesn't work out, I'll have no choice but to leave the City. How embarrassing. Twenty-four and living with my parents in the 'burbs? No, thank you.

"Oh god," I mutter, tugging on the too-small skirt that's protesting the curve of my hips. "I look like a hooker."

"Whaaat?" The dressing room doorknob rattles and Tessa hollers through the wall. "Come on, open up. Let me see."

"Oh, hell no. It's bad." Worse than bad, it's atrocious. Of all the clothing lines owned by Evans, Roth and Sloane, this one had the most potential. Even the poster on the changing room wall says the clothes will create *Beauty from every angle*. I scoff. Not the angle of *my* ass.

Henry Sloane is hot as shit, but he's a fucking liar. His clothing line is no different from the rest of the stores we've been to. Too small. Too expensive. Too exclusive for anyone who's not born of the Manhattan elite.

A suit-clad Sloane stares back at me through the photo on the wall, his arm around a model so thin I imagine her clothes are necessary to hide her rib cage. Her cheekbones poke out of her unnaturally perfect face, and I can't help but feel sorry for her. She must live on liquid nutrition to keep that figure.

"I like food too much to ever look like that," I mutter, pulling at the fabric of the skirt. "I need to go on a diet."

"Hannah, no. They're all crap. Low carb, low fat, low calorie, it doesn't matter. You'll be miserable. What can I do? Can I get you another size?" Tessa asks, her voice full of sympathy.

I stare at my reflection, crisp white cotton stretching across my chest, buttons straining against the tiny threads that hold them in place. "Nah. I give up. We should head back. Remind me to buy celery on the way home, would you?" I should have known that high-end stores only cater to the rich and model-thin.

"Seriously, Hannah. It's not you, it's the clothes."

Tessa means well, but the declaration only stokes the smoldering frustration in my chest. "Yeah, well, what am I gonna do? I need to look professional. I can't go to Evans, Roth and Sloane in *this*." In one swift motion, I swing the dressing room door open and let it bang against the wall.

Tessa's lips round into an O before she fights a losing battle with her smile. "It's not as bad as you think."

"Liar."

"Okay, so it's a little tight." She taps on her phone before holding it out in front of her. "Hold on, let's ask Vi. She'll tell it like it is." Tessa swipes at the screen and holds it up to her face. "Hey, honey. We need your opinion."

One more tap and she points the phone at me.

I give Tessa's girlfriend a half-hearted wave. "If I skip dinner, you think this blouse will fit me in the morning?"

Even on the tiny screen, I catch the moment Violet takes in what I'm wearing. "Oh, wow." She blows out a breath. "You didn't tell me your new boss was a pimp."

I point a finger at Tessa. "Dammit, I told you!"

She scrunches up her face. "I'm sorry. You know I love you." Turning the screen toward herself, she says, "Please tell her it's just the stupid brand."

With the phone pointed back at me, Violet nods. "She's right. You've got a great bod, Hannah. Where the heck are you guys, anyway?"

"Fifth Avenue," Tessa says. "Sloane's."

"Sloane's? Oooh, I heard the lingerie is to die for."

I tug on the teal strap of the bra I'm trying on. "Well, I about died when I saw the price of this." Too bad it's the only thing that's fit me all day. "I just wish I could figure out why all these designers make their bras for people with big boobs, but the shirts for prepubescent teens." I cup my hands around my breasts. "I'm barely a C-cup, and this blouse is ready to blow."

Tessa giggles and the phone shakes in her hand.

I stretch my arms to prove my point, and the blouse makes an ominous noise that's dangerously close to a tear. I freeze. "Oh, shit," I whisper.

My eyes meet Tessa's, and a snicker sneaks past her firmly-pressed lips.

I grin. "Laugh all you want, I'm one deep breath away from pelting you with buttons."

On the screen, Violet's expression turns serious. "It's really not funny if you think about it. All these hoity-toity designers make their clothes for double-zero models. It's no wonder they cost so much, they exclude ninety-nine percent of the population. I bet that shirt doesn't even go up to an eight."

"You're right," I tell her. "This is the biggest one, and it's a six. Tomorrow I'm going on a diet."

"See," she shrieks. "These companies need to know that what they're doing is not only hypocritical, but it's also damaging to society. Am I right?"

I nod as I brace myself for another tirade. Vi's all about social injustice and holding brands accountable.

"Think about it. Before today, I've never heard you utter the D-word."

"Uhh, she says dick all the time," Tessa interrupts.

"Not dick—*diet*. A few hours on Fifth Avenue, and you've

resigned yourself to eating like a rabbit."

"It wouldn't hurt me to shed a couple of pounds." I bet most women feel the same after a day of shopping.

"No! Why aren't you pissed?" Vi yells. "I'm not even there, and I'm furious for you."

Tessa grimaces and motions for me to agree with her girlfriend.

"I *am* angry," I say. "And I don't care how hot Sloane looks in his fancy suit. He can kiss my ass if he thinks I'll go broke for one of these over-priced scraps of fabric."

"Yes!" Violet shouts.

Tessa gives me a thumbs up and nods for me to keep going.

"And, uhhh…He ought to stick to what he knows and stop designing clothes for people who don't have dicks." The charms on my bracelet jingle as I grab at my crotch for added emphasis.

"Exactly!"

"Better yet, I hope everyone boycotts his stupid brand and he goes bankrupt. That'll teach him!"

"Excuse me?"

My head whips around to find a salesperson standing in the doorway of the fitting area.

She points at Tessa's phone. "Put that away. No cameras allowed back here."

"Oh, crap." I beeline back into the changing room and close the door as Tessa mutters a quick goodbye to Violet. "I think I took that a little too far," I tell her through the wall.

"Nah, you're good."

"You're right about one thing though," I say, unbuttoning the blouse.

"Yeah? What's that?"

"I really do say dick a lot."

Tess snickers. "Yeah, but it's always warranted."

With the blouse back on its hanger, I admire the pretty teal bra. It's actually very flattering. "This bra makes my boobs look fantastic," I call out. "Maybe I could splurge on just this one little thing."

"No bra is worth four hundred dollars."

I sigh. Goddamn Tessa and her voice of reason.

***

On the fifty-second floor of an office tower in Manhattan, I sit tucked away in my cube working on a magazine ad that's due by the end of the week. I have no doubt I'll make the deadline, but there's no time to waste. My first few days at Evans, Roth and Sloane have been more exciting than the slog of meaningless tasks I'd expected. More accurately, I've been tossed in the deep end—and I love it.

According to my boss, Kyle, his division has been desperate for another designer for months. He's busting his ass with HR to make the position permanent, but they won't make that decision until next quarter's numbers come out. Until then, he said he's grateful to have someone to offload some of the backlog.

Kyle sets another folder in the already overflowing inbox on my desk. "Sorry, Hannah. I've got one more project for you. Should be pretty straightforward, and the client doesn't need the digital assets until next week."

Nodding, I flip the folder open and skim the spec sheet. "I'll get a draft to you tomorrow."

"Perfect." Kyle begins to walk away but turns and comes back to my desk. "Did you get the invite for the team meeting this afternoon?"

I double-check my email and shake my head. I spent a good hour this morning setting up folders and rules for the emails that started flooding my inbox. There was definitely no meeting invite.

Kyle's brow furrows in concentration as he types on his phone. "There. It's sent. It's at three in Boardroom Two. Don't act surprised when I put you on the spot and introduce you to the rest of the department."

The meeting request appears on my screen, and I click to accept it. "Looking forward to it."

He taps my desk. "Great. That's what I like to hear."

***

With two minutes to spare, I slide into one of the few remaining seats in the boardroom and inspect my blouse to make sure it isn't gaping. Thanks to Tessa's overflowing closet, I have a few key pieces of clothing to get me through the week, but I'm not taking any chances when it comes to workplace wardrobe malfunctions.

Around the crowded table, men and women I haven't met flip through the stacks of paper in front of them. I pick up the first few booklets in my pile and skim through the titles. A competitive analysis for a proposed new perfume line, a business case to roll out the product before mid-year, and a marketing plan for Henry Sloane's latest ad campaign.

Excitement bubbles through me. If I'm promoted to full-time, it could be *my* designs hanging on the walls of Sloane's Fifth Avenue store. His clothing line would be my dream portfolio. Tiny pangs of guilt stab at my chest for what I said the other day. I don't *actually* want him to go bankrupt.

In the midst of my musing, the boardroom door bursts open.

As if summoned by my reverie, Henry Sloane appears in the doorway, his cell phone pressed against his ear. *"Can't* does not exist in my vocabulary," he growls. "Make it go away." He taps on his phone without a goodbye and peers around the table. "Let's get started."

Eerie silence replaces the hum of pre-meeting chatter as Henry steps away from the door. It swings closed behind him, and I lose track of what he's saying. My eyes remain locked on the massive number three that's etched into the frosted glass of Boardroom Two.

My stomach sinks into my borrowed Jimmy Choos.

Oh shit. Wrong boardroom.

Without thinking, I jump to my feet.

"Sit down!"

My ass plants itself back into the plush leather chair at the command. I don't need a visual to know the words are meant for me. Swiveling to face the front of the room, I slowly meet the angry stare of the most beautiful pair of blue eyes I've ever seen. They stand out against Henry's dark brown hair like beacons of aquamarine.

My breath catches in my throat, and I choke out a quiet *sorry* without bothering to explain that I'm not meant to be here.

"Sir?" A young woman taps his arm, seemingly unfazed by his irritable mood. "Here's your agenda."

"Fuck the agenda," he grumbles.

Even though he's dismissed it, I take a copy of the agenda from the pile being passed around and hand the rest to the person beside me.

"You."

My head snaps up to find Henry staring me down again. I

brace myself for public humiliation. He's probably figured out that I'm an imposter.

"Rip it up."

"Huh?" My gaze bounces back and forth between him and the agenda.

His brow furrows deeper as if my confusion isn't warranted. "You heard me. Rip. It. Up."

Glancing around the table, I'm grateful for the silent piece of advice that comes in the form of a slow nod from the older gentleman sitting across from me. With measured movement, I hold the paper out in front of me.

And then I tear it in half.

Amplified by the silent room, the ripping echoes like a squealing baby during evening prayer. I grit my teeth and force my eyes up to meet Henry's.

"Good. Now we're all on the same page." He scans the room, pausing on each person as if ensuring he's got everyone's attention. "Right now, I don't give a flying fuck about marketing or product launches." He picks up a wireless remote from the table. "Pam, get the lights."

His young assistant scurries to the back of the room, and the lights fade to a muted glow. The projector flickers into focus, and headlines from various news articles fill the screen.

Henry sighs. "Public calls for boycott of new fashion line by Henry Sloane." Click. "Evans, Roth and Sloane face criticism over new elitist clothes." Click. "NYSE: ERS stock plunges amidst launch of controversial clothing."

Slide after slide, the headlines change, all of them equally bad. "Protest planned as fury grows over designer exclusion." Click. "Oh, yes. Here's a good one." A doctored corporate headshot of Henry fills the screen with several hashtags stamped at the bottom, and a crudely-drawn penis pointed at his mouth. "Who'd like to read these hashtags aloud? Gerald?"

The older gentleman across from me clears his throat. "Hashtag… uh… stick to dicks. Hashtag boycott Sloane."

"Thank you. And, the video that started it all. Let's watch, shall we?" Henry clicks the remote again and a circular icon whirls in the middle of the screen.

I peer around the table. Judging from the expressions on all the other faces, this is not what anyone else was expecting either.

"…I'm barely a C-cup, and this blouse is ready to blow."

My head snaps to the front of the room at the sound of my voice, and I stifle a gasp with my palm as my ill-clad body comes into view.

Under the shield of darkness, I draw long, slow breaths to keep from passing out. This is bad. Oh god, this is worse than bad. I'm in deep, deep shit.

CHAPTER *two*

Amid my silent panic, a bright light clouds my vision, and for a moment, I accept my fate. I've well and truly died of embarrassment. And dammit, I deserve it.

Unfortunately for me, Pam's just turned the boardroom lights back on, and it's taking me a second to adjust. I'm still stuck here with my boss's boss's boss who just saw me half-naked ranting about his clothing line. If there was ever a perfect time for the Earth to swallow me up, it's now. Please, God, do me a solid and make me self-combust. And while you're at it, send Vi along for the ride. This stunt reeks of her social activism bullshit.

At the front of the room, Henry pauses the video when it starts to replay and sets the remote back on the table. On screen, my hands are frozen, cupped obscenely around my breasts while the blouse looks comically ready to bust open.

If I owe Violet even an ounce of mercy for what she's done, it's that she had the decency to blur my face.

"So?" Henry asks. "Thoughts?"

That's what I want to know. What the hell was Vi thinking?

Beneath the table, I wring my fingers and pray my face is neither pale as death nor red as Henry's tie. The key to getting out of here unscathed is to go unnoticed.

On the far side of the room, a preppy-looking guy rocks back in his chair, pushing his fingers through his hair as if Sloane's making a big deal out of nothing. "PR says there's no such thing as bad publicity."

I blow out the breath I've been holding. Preppy Guy is right. Sweep it under the rug and move on. Nobody cares about some idiot in too-small clothes.

"I disagree," Gerald says, his English accent catching me off guard. "In this digital age, something as simple as a tweet can crush the integrity of a brand. How we respond to this could make or break us."

Fuck, Gerald, why are you doing this to me? I slump back in my chair. Maybe living in the 'burbs won't be so bad. Oh, man, who am I kidding? The last time I went home, Mom asked for my advice on drumming up clients for her ear candling business. She just doesn't understand. There's no untapped market for lymphatic drainage.

"I agree with Doug," the woman beside me says, referring to my preppy friend. "This girl's a nobody. She's just mad she can't fit into the clothes."

"She probably drinks too many Frappuccinos," someone else pipes up. "Those things are loaded with sugar."

It's not the sugar that keeps me away. "She can't afford

Frappuccinos," I mutter.

"Pardon?" Crossing his arms over his chest, Henry peers at me, his brows pulled into a mighty deep V. Someone ought to tell him he's going to need Botox before he's thirty if he keeps that up.

"Nothing," I grumble.

He stares at me, and I meet him dagger for dagger, hoping my act of fearlessness will force him to move on to someone else.

It works. But it also lights a fire between my legs. That smoldering expression matches the one in his very first ad campaign. It might have been five years ago, but it's impossible to forget. I could have written a thesis paper on that look alone.

Henry turns to Gerald. "What do you propose we do?"

"Simple," he says. "Find out who this woman is. Find out who's behind this defamation and threaten legal action."

I stifle a gasp and clench my fists. No, no, no. Goddammit, Gerald.

Henry stares me down again and damn, that fierceness in his eyes is hot as hell. "Do you have something to add?"

I shake my head and try to pull myself together. This is serious. I shouldn't be thinking of the chiseled body hiding beneath his suit.

He tips his head to the side, goading me. "Go on, you look about ready to burst."

Somewhere down the table somebody snickers, no doubt from Sloane's double entendre.

And just like that, my switch flips from frisky to goddamn furious. All these execs talking smack unknowingly in front of me. Henry Sloane has the power to blacklist me from every business in the state, but I don't care. These people don't know shit about marketing. They're telling him what he wants to hear, but it's time to cut the crap. "Legal action won't solve anything," I tell him. "It's only going to make you look like a hardass." Not to mention, you can't take money from a pauper. Most months I'm in the red.

"I *am* a hardass."

"I mean—" I draw a steady breath. "Maybe there's some truth to her frustration."

A dozen heads turn in my direction.

Fuck, Hannah, way to go unnoticed. I grit my teeth. There's no going back now. "It's just… your slogan says the clothes will create *Beauty from every angle.* Not only is that misleading, but it's also condescending."

"Condescending *how?*" Henry pins me in place with his intense blue eyes.

"Because it implies that women need your clothes to look beautiful. And since your clothing line doesn't go past a six—" I shrug "—anyone who isn't that small can't possibly be beautiful."

Henry's brows pull together once again, and he steps closer, examining my face. His cologne circles around me, the masculine scent as powerful and intoxicating as his presence. "Who are you?"

Oh shit. In all the horror that's unfolded in the past few minutes, I'd forgotten that I'm not even meant to be here. I draw another calming breath. "I'm Hannah O'Keefe. I thought this was Boardroom Two."

Henry ponders my statement. "I see." He points at the door. "Thank you, Hannah. You can go now."

With an obedient nod, I gather my pen and notepad. "Yes, sir. Sorry for the mix-up." Not sorry for speaking up. At least, not yet.

***

Back at my desk, I try reading through the emails that arrived while I was ending my career, but the words all blur together. As soon as Henry's legal team tracks down Vi's account, there'll be a clear link to me. And even if they don't, one look at the security footage from Sloane's store and I'm done. It's only a matter of time before I'm found out.

At ten to three, I join Kyle and the rest of the team in the real Boardroom Two, directly across from Sloane's meeting. He and his execs are still hard at work, and judging by the murmuring around our boardroom table, news has spread about the viral video that's causing Sloane a headache.

"All right, team," Kyle starts. "I'll keep this short, so we can move on with the remainder of our Thursday." He points to me. "For those of you who haven't had the chance to meet the newest member of our team, this is Hannah O'Keefe. She'll be doing the graphic design on some of our smaller portfolios until she gets her feet wet. Hannah is a recent graduate of our very own NYU. She has her Master's in Marketing Communications, and I think she'll fit right in here."

"Thank you," I say, forcing what I hope is a convincing smile. "I'm looking forward to working with you all." Although, the way my day is going, it might only be for a few more hours.

Around the table, I'm met with nods and welcomes, and I try to relax into my chair.

"So," Kyle blurts. "The other thing I'd like to touch on before we dive into today's agenda is the marketing fiasco

Sloane's new line of clothing is facing. How many of you know what I'm talking about?"

A chorus of yeses and several snickers circle the room, and I nod along with the group. Kyle breaks into a spiel about how marketing can go wrong, pointing out that even brands as big as Sloane's aren't immune to the power of social media. At last, he moves on to other topics, and a little over an hour later, he calls the meeting to a close.

As we file out of the room, the door to Boardroom Three opens up, and the executive team begins to leave. Gerald shares a sympathetic smile as he passes, and I nod in acknowledgement even though I ought to kick his ass for wanting to sue me.

Behind Gerald, and standing a foot taller, Henry eyes me warily. Pretending I don't see him, I drop my head and focus on moving one foot in front of the other. Under the weight of his heady stare, I continue down the hallway. It's not until I'm safely back in my cubicle that I'm finally able to breathe.

***

By the time I get home to the crappy apartment I share with Tessa and Vi, my head is pounding, and all the emotion that's been bubbling under the surface comes pouring out.

I rush toward the bedroom Vi shares with Tessa and burst through the door without bothering to knock. She'll be up for work soon, anyway. "How could you?" I shout.

Vi bolts upright in bed and rubs her eyes. "Huh? What?"

"You *know* what, Vi! The video!" Hot, wet tears blur my vision, and I swipe them away with the back of my hand. "I'm going to get fired. I can't believe you'd do something so... so selfish."

"Hang on a minute." Vi swings her legs over the side of the bed and stands beside it. Naked.

With my hand in front of my face, I block her from my view. "Ugh. Dammit, Vi. Put something on."

"I am. Jesus." She slips a tie-dyed maxi dress over her head. "Start again. What video?"

"The one you took of me at Sloane's," I shriek. "It's all over the internet!"

Her eyes round into saucers as realization dawns on her face. "Ohhh."

I grit my teeth. "Yeah. Ohhh."

Vi steps toward me, her palms raised out in front of her. "I just shared it with a couple of friends," she says. "Two, three max." Suddenly, she grimaces, and I brace myself for another blow. "And, I might have posted it in one of my online groups." She rushes to her laptop. "I'm so sorry. I'll take it down right now. I just thought it was another perfect example of how celebrity brands are demoralizing to society."

Flopping back onto her unmade bed, I stare at the ceiling. "It's too late, Vi. It's gone viral."

"No, it can't have. It's only been a couple of days." She whistles. "Oh, wow. This post has nine hundred thousand views."

Drawing a shaky breath, I roll over to grab a tissue from Vi's nightstand and blow my nose.

"Oh, Hannah," she whispers. "I'm so sorry. Does your boss know?"

"About the video, yes. That it's me? No, not yet. Oh god, what am I gonna do?"

Vi hums. "Maybe tomorrow there'll be something else that's

gone viral, and the video will be old news."

"True. I could pretend I don't know anything and hope it goes away." I scrunch up my face. That won't work. "I doubt Henry Sloane will forget about it any time soon. I sat in a meeting with him today."

"Whaaaaat?" Her voice jumps an octave as she moves across the room to sit beside me. "*How?*"

"It's a long story," I tell her, tossing the dirty tissue in her wastebasket.

"Is he as gorgeous as he is in his ads, or are they mostly airbrushed?" She shakes her head. "Ah, who am I kidding, of course they're airbrushed. All ads are full of lies."

"Oh, he doesn't need much airbrushing," I say. "He's damn near perfect."

Vi lies back on the bed, and sighs. "Of course, he is. Does he have any sisters?"

With a quiet laugh, I collapse back onto the mattress and turn my head toward my friend. "He was so mad today. Like raging, furious, mad."

"Really?"

"Yeah. It was so fucking hot," I admit.

She grins. "I can't believe you know Henry Sloane."

I sigh. "I don't. Not really. Anyway, it doesn't matter. I doubt I'll have a job tomorrow."

Vi's smile falls from her face. "I'm really sorry, Hannah. For everything. I don't think there's anything I can do, but tell me if there is. I'll make sure the video gets removed."

"At least you blurred my face out. So there's that."

"Huh?" Vi's brows draw together. "What do you mean? I didn't blur anything."

That little tidbit takes a second to sink in. "Oh god," I breathe, sitting up on the bed. "Oh shit. Oh fuck."

Violet follows suit, jack-knifing to a seated position. "What? What is it? I'm so confused right now."

Grabbing her hand, I stare into her hazel eyes and implore her to take a fucking hint. "If you didn't blur my face, that means there're copies of the video floating around that show *who I am*!"

She hums. "So, whoever posted the video must have blurred it first?"

I nod.

"And they can see who you are?"

I nod again.

"And other people could still share the video I posted that isn't blurred?"

I love her, but she can be a total ditz sometimes. "Yes, Violet! Oh my god! You need to delete it!"

CHAPTER three

After scouring the internet for hours last night, I'm fairly confident the only video making the rounds is the one that has my face blurred. Still, knowing the other one is floating around out there makes me a little uneasy. But if I take one thing away from this fiasco, it's that online comments are best ignored. Nothing good can come from reading them. Scattered within all the funny memes and anger at Henry Sloane are little pokes at me. There's only so many chubby hooker jokes a girl can take before she swears off food forever. So far, I've skipped breakfast *and* lunch, and now, I can barely focus on my work.

"Hannah?"

I jerk back in my chair, covering my heart with my hand as I spin around to face Henry's assistant outside my cube. "Oh! You scared me."

"Sorry." Pam's tight-lipped smile does nothing to calm my

nerves. "Would you come with me, please? Henry Sloane would like to see you in his office."

Standing, I peer over her shoulder and look for signs of security. Everyone I know who's ever been fired has been let go at the end of the day. I glance down at my watch. Ten to five on a Friday afternoon? Yeah, I'm totally getting axed.

Staying a step behind, I follow Pam down the hallway, discreetly admiring her outfit. The form-fitting dress is from Sloane's on Fifth, no doubt. I recognize the stunning shade of steel gray. "Am I in trouble?"

"No."

I sigh. Thank god. "Do you know why he wants to see me?"

Pam's flashy heels click loudly on the polished floor as she speeds up her pace. "He didn't say."

Clearly not one for small talk, I try another tactic to get Pam to open up. "I like your shoes." For all I know, they're last season's, but somehow I doubt it. Like the rest of her outfit, Pam's red-soled pumps scream big money. My simple black dress pales in comparison, but at least it didn't put me into debt.

As if I've injected her with a dose of bubbly schoolgirl, Pam's expression morphs into one of delight. "OMG. Aren't they the cutest? I bought them last week." She sighs dramatically. "Every time I visit Louboutin, I can't help but treat myself."

Ignoring the fact that I've been saying Louboutin wrong my entire life, I try to keep the momentum of our conversation going. If I can get an in with Pam and her friends, I might stand a chance at making my contract permanent. Like Tessa always says, it's all in who you know and who you blow. "They're fabulous," I gush. "So versatile."

Pam stops and peers down at the ancient Jimmy Choos I borrowed from Tessa. "Yours are nice, too."

"Oh, these old things? Nah. They're just my backups. I snapped a heel on my Manolo Blahnik's the other day. I've never cried so hard," I lie.

Pam clutches her chest. "Oh no! That's terrible. I know a repair guy on West Fifty-Fifth who's fabulous. I'll email you his address."

"You're amazing, Pam, thank you." I force a smile. I'm such a fraud. At some point she's gonna want to see those pricey shoes—and then what?

At the end of the hallway, Pam knocks on the double oak doors and pokes her head inside. "Mr. Sloane, I have Miss O'Keefe here for you."

Beyond the threshold, Henry's muffled response is met with a nod from Pam. She pulls the heavy door open the rest of the way. "Go on in. He's just finishing up a call."

"Thanks, Pam." Nervous flutters attack my stomach, but I battle back with calming breaths. It's no big deal. I'm not in trouble, and even if I am, I stand behind my words. I did nothing wrong. Yes—let's go with that.

"Hannah?"

Pam's quiet voice snaps me out my pep talk and propels me into motion. I square my shoulders and step into the illustrious world of the one percent.

Sloane's office smells just like him. A mix of his cologne and leather and exorbitant amounts of wealth. It's no wonder his name is synonymous with success. Everything around him exudes power and luxury.

"Tough shit, Evans. You'll have to wait 'til Monday. I've got more things to do than I have hours."

My head snaps up at the sudden burst of Henry's voice. From behind his desk, he points to one of the leather chairs in front of him, and I take his silent cue to sit.

Staring everywhere but at him, I try to stay focused. Whomever he's talking to is getting an earful, and I have a feeling that I'll be next. And as hot as Henry is when he's angry, I'd rather not be on the receiving end of his wicked mouth.

Unless it's to kiss me.

Mmmm. I sneak a glance at him. It's easy to see why he's the face of his iconic brand. No model in existence has their pout perfected like Henry Sloane. I'd bet my share of rent those lips have mastered the art of the whisper-soft kiss.

"They have," Henry says out of nowhere.

I suck in a quiet breath. Oh crap. Did I say that out loud?

"But they can wait until the report is ready like everybody else," he continues, still on his phone call.

Jesus. I relax into the chair. That was close.

Dropping my gaze, I try to keep my mind off Sloane and how sexy he looks with a scowl. Surely, the man must have some flaws. Judging by the clusterfuck he calls his desk, he's no Mr. Clean. File folders scatter the polished surface along with loose papers and sticky notes all over the place. In a way, I feel sorry for the guy. He's clearly busy. But the other side of me— the neat-freak part—knows he'd get more done if he was better organized. I bet he's a procrastinator, too. God, I'd hate to see his email inbox.

With the exception of his desk, the rest of Henry's office is surprisingly immaculate. Groups of furniture break up the vastness of the space, creating intimate sitting areas around the room. On one side, floor-to-ceiling bookshelves line the wall behind a six-person table, and on the other, two leather wingback chairs face a matching loveseat in front of a breathtaking view of the city.

Henry leans back in his chair and taps his fancy silver pen against his bottom lip. "Hmm. Yes, that should work," he says. Tap. Tap. "Yeah, I'll write it down. Tuesday night at nine." Tap. Tap. Tap.

I try to follow his one-sided conversation, but soon, I'm enthralled by his tapping, by the way his tongue sneaks out to wet his lips, and by the quiet hums that come between his answers. God, what is it about Henry Sloane that's so enticing? Certainly not his sunny disposition.

But he is undeniably easy on the eyes. Classically handsome, refined yet rough in all the right places. Like his jaw.

Tap.

Mmmm. That five o'clock shadow.

"I have to go," he says. Tap.

Tap.

God, it's been too long since I felt the gentle scrape of scruff between my thighs.

Tap.

Tap.

My eyes flick up to Henry's.

Shit.

His phone is back in its cradle, and his focus is on me.

"Miss O'Keefe."

Oh crap. This is it. I sit up straighter and clear my head of every indecent thought. "Hi." Hi? *Hi?* Jesus, Hannah.

Sloane stares at me, his expression an equal mix of

confusion and unamused. "Hi."

I grimace. "I'm sorry. I'm the queen of crappy first impressions."

"The queen of crappy second impressions, too."

My face scrunches again. "You're right. I'm so sorry about that. I got the meeting rooms mixed up with the times and—"

Henry holds up his hand, and my mouth snaps shut.

"My first instinct was to fire you," he blurts.

My head bobs involuntarily. "I understand. I shouldn't have spoken out at the meeting... I shouldn't have even been there."

"True." He taps his pen against his lips before pointing it at me. "But you were right."

"I was?"

"Unfortunately." He sets his silver pen down on a pile of paper and for some reason that disappoints me. "I don't often admit to being wrong," he adds. "But in this case, I might be."

"That's great news."

His brow furrows.

"Because now you can fix it," I clarify. "So many people wouldn't. It's commendable."

"Who said I'm going to fix it?"

"You're not?" I fight to keep a neutral tone. "You just said that you were wrong."

"Yes, but that doesn't mean I need to take action. My team has assured me that this will all blow over." He waves a hand as if the simple motion will wipe the video from existence. "By Monday it will be long forgotten."

Stunned, I sit in silence. Vi was right. People like him don't give a damn about morals. He cares about his bottom line. Period.

I stand from the chair, preparing to get the hell out before my building outrage spills from my mouth and gets me in deeper trouble. "If that's all, I should get going."

Sloane peers at his watch. "Yes, I'm sorry for keeping you. I wanted you to know that I appreciate the courage it must have taken to speak out against a room full of execs."

"Not that it matters," I mutter. I was naive to think he'd see the error of his ways and want to do better.

"You seem upset."

"I'm fine." I unclench my jaw before I break a tooth. The last thing I need is an emergency trip to the dentist.

His mouth begins to twitch as if he's holding back a smile. "I've never met a woman who says she's fine and means it."

Under normal circumstances, an almost smile from Sloane would make me swoon, but not right now.

He crosses his arms over his chest, and the fabric of his dress shirt pulls tight against his pecks. He tips his head toward me. "Well? Don't be shy. I'm not going to fire you."

I sigh. "I'm a little frustrated."

"At me?"

Before thinking better of it, I shrug.

Henry rounds his desk, so we're face to face. Broad shoulders fill his suit, but it's his height that feels imposing. He stands at least a head taller than my five-foot-seven stature and even as he sits on the edge of his desk, we're still not eye-to-eye.

"Why are you frustrated, Hannah?"

The gentle sound of my name on his lips sends goosebumps rolling down my arms. In the back of my mind, I consider telling him everything. That it's me in the video, that Vi posted it online, and that it was never my intention to harm his company's image.

Against my better judgement, I share a half-truth. "The girl in the video... I've been there. I understand her frustration with clothing lines like yours. No offense."

"None taken. Go on."

"Finding clothes to fit our bodies is a challenge. We all have curves in different places—or none. At the end of the day, we all just want to feel good in our skin. We want to feel beautiful." Glancing away, I take a deep breath and dig up the courage I need to really drill my message home. "I feel like I'm pretty average. Not fat, not overly skinny."

As if assessing my statement, Henry's blue eyes rake over my body. I stamp down the flutters in my stomach before they give me false hope. Men like Henry Sloane don't fall for women like me. They fall for women like Pam. Women who fit into a two and know how to say Louboutin.

"Your new line of women's clothing is gorgeous. The perfect blend of professional and trendy." Biting my lip, I meet his gaze before delivering the final embarrassing blow. "But they would never fit me."

Heat crawls up my face as I fight tears I didn't realize were forming. I will not cry. Not over something as stupid as clothes.

"I see," he says, clearing his throat. "I'm sorry to hear that."

With nothing else to add, an awkward stretch of silence builds between us.

"I really do need to get going," I say, looking toward the bank of windows. The sun is falling lower in the sky, and by the time I'm home, I'll be lucky if it isn't dark.

"Yes, of course. Can I call you a cab?"

I shake my head and give him a small smile. "No, thank you, Mr. Sloane. I'm fine."

***

As I expected, the sun has all but set over New York City when I emerge from underground. Even at a quick clip, it's a good twenty-minute walk from the subway to my apartment door. It's the leg of my commute I least look forward to, not just because my feet are well past aching, but because I know too well what dangers could be lurking in the alleys.

At the entrance of my building, I fiddle with the key in the lock, silently cursing the ancient contraption until it lets me open the door.

"Hey!"

Spinning around, I clutch my purse to my chest.

"Thank god, you're here," Tessa says, squeezing through the gap before the door can close. "My arms are going to fall off." She shoves an overstuffed canvas bag in my direction. "Thanks. You're a gem."

I grab the bag and scoff. "You're lucky. Sloane kept me late."

"Oh yeah? How come?"

We slog our way up three flights of stairs as I tell her about my meeting with Henry.

"So that's it?" Tessa drops her bags on the floor inside our apartment. "What a dick."

Vi appears from the hallway and kisses Tessa on the cheek. "Who's a dick?"

"Sloane." I drop the bag I'm carrying beside the rest. "He told me I was right about his clothing line, but he's not going to change it."

"What a dick," Vi echoes. "Did he say why?"

"His *team* says it's all going to blow over. There's no reason to spend the time or money."

Vi shakes her head. "They underestimate the power of social media. Rookie mistake."

"Maybe it's for the best," I say. "I'm happy to forget this ever happened and not get fired—or sued."

"He can't sue you," Tessa says. "Any judge would throw the case out. Besides, you did nothing wrong."

I lean against the wall and slip off my heels. "Maybe. But he could fire me. And he could make it really, really hard for me to get another job."

Violet taps my arm. "Don't worry, it won't come to that. I sent another message to my online group this morning. I asked them to delete any copies of the video from their feeds. Most of them were supportive and said they would."

"Most?"

"Well…" She scrunches up her face as if looking for the right words. "…a few were asking questions." She holds up her hand. "But don't worry, I told them how important this is to you. That it could cost you your job."

"You told them I work for Evans, Roth and Sloane? Vi! What were you thinking?"

"No, no. Not all of them, just one or two. It's fine. Look—" She reaches into her pocket and pulls out her phone. "Suzie said *sure, no problem.* Mark said *consider it done.*" Vi's phone beeps as she peers at the screen and her brows pull together the longer she stares at it.

"What is it?" Dread pools in the pit of my stomach as her face pales to a sullen gray. "Vi?"

She draws a deep breath before meeting my gaze. "He must be joking. I don't recognize this guy. Davis. No last name. He says he'll take the video down, but it'll cost us ten grand if we don't want it sent to Henry Sloane."

CHAPTER four

Tessa and I huddle around Vi and her phone in the middle of our tiny living room.

"We should play it cool," Tessa says. "Pretend we don't care."

"Too late," I groan. "He already knows we care, otherwise, he wouldn't be trying to extort us."

Tessa steps away from the group and flops down on the couch. "Why are you friends with these people, Vi? I get that you want to save the world and shit, but come on. They're nuts."

"*Passionate*," Vi counters. "They're very passionate. And mostly harmless."

"Except for Davis." He's batshit crazy. I sit down on the couch beside Tessa and curl my legs beneath me. "We need to buy some time. Tell him we don't have ten thousand."

She taps on her phone. "Done. I said, *sorry pal, we ain't got shit.*"

"Dammit, Vi, don't provoke him," I say. "Give him my cell number and tell him to call me. People aren't as ballsy over the phone."

Violet nods, and a few minutes later, my phone chimes with an incoming message. It's from an unknown number, but it's definitely Davis.

$10K or prep your resume. Your choice.

I tap out a quick reply.

I don't have that much lying around. I need more time.

His response lights up my screen.

You've got 2 weeks. I want the first $3K by next week or else.

I have a better chance of fucking Sloane than finding ten grand. Davis is gonna have to wait.

Four weeks. And I'll get you $2K by next week. That's the best I can do.

I'm not even sure *that's* possible. I'm going to need a miracle to pull this off.

Dots tumble along the bottom of the screen as I wait with bated breath for Davis's message to appear.

Fine. A second late or a dollar short and you can kiss your hoity-toity job goodbye.

"Ugh. Fuck you, Davis." I toss my phone onto the table and give it the finger. "Why me?"

"We should call the police," Tessa suggests. "Maybe they would make him turn over the video."

Oh, sweet Tessa, if only it were that easy. I flop back on the couch and groan. "I don't think it works like that. The video was shared to a public group. It'll never truly be gone."

"You shouldn't give him a single cent," she says. "He could take it all and send the video to Sloane anyway."

I stare at the stark-white ceiling. "I know."

"Or he could just keep asking for more and more money," she adds.

"I know." My fate is in the hands of a stranger, but it's the only viable option I've got.

"Or—"

"I know, Tessa. *I know*. You're completely right on all counts. I have no reason to trust him."

"But you're going to pay him anyway," Tessa says, her shoulders slumping.

"Yeah. I am." I huff a bitter laugh. Only time will tell if I'm making a mistake. "Anyone have a couple thousand dollars I can borrow?"

Violet clears her throat. "Um, I have some money you can have."

Tessa sits up straight up and stares dumbfounded at her girlfriend. Between the three of us, Vi's the thriftiest and always claims she's broke.

Violet pads down the hallway toward the bedroom she shares with Tessa, and returns with a giant plastic water jug full of small bills and change.

"Tips," she says, setting it on the carpet. "I've been saving for a while. There's probably four or five hundred at least."

Standing from the couch, I walk over to Vi and pull her into a bear hug. "Oh, Vi. I can't take your tips." She's always complaining about how little she's paid at the dive bar where she and Tessa work the late shift.

"Please take it," she begs. "This is all my fault."

Tessa nods at me like I'd be a fool to say no.

As much as I hate owing people money, my desperation outweighs my pride. "I'll pay you back," I say to Vi. "I promise."

***

By the time Monday rolls around, I'm confident I can meet Davis's first installment without too much trouble. Vi's tip jar held a whopping six-hundred and twenty-seven dollars and eighteen subway tokens. She said I could keep those, too. Add in my first paycheck, and by Friday, I'll have more than enough to cover the initial payment.

Beyond that, things get tricky. If I max out my credit cards and give Davis my paychecks, I'll have no money left to live on. But if I don't pay Davis, he'll send the video to Sloane, and I'll lose my job—leaving me no money to live on. Either way, I'm fucked.

The only good thing that's come of this video nightmare is the weight loss. I'm too broke to stress-eat, and the bulk of my diet is celery. Ironically, it's the easiest five pounds I've ever dropped.

I stare at the conglomerate of muffins on the lunchroom table and try not to salivate. In my financial state, I should be smuggling those suckers home in my handbag, but I opt for coffee instead. Evans, Roth and Sloane doesn't cheap out on their employees. I choose a specialty blend with Hazelnut and pour the last of it into my mug.

Gerald steps up beside me and looks over the flavored coffee dispensers. "Oh, bloody hell," he huffs. "No Hazelnut again. That's twice now."

I peer down at my mug but think better of telling Gerald I'm responsible for his latest coffee woes.

"Looks like Hannah got the last of it." The smooth silk of Henry's voice caresses my ear as he leans in close and pretends to peek into my cup.

Gerald eyes my mug before turning back to the coffee choices. He mutters under his breath about rubbish flavors, but it's too hard to make out the meaning of his English cuss words. I'm pretty sure I'm on his shit list now.

I glower at Henry and whisper, "Thanks for throwing me under the bus."

He grins at me, and it takes all my strength to not drop my mug. It changes his entire appearance. His smoldering deep-set eyes twinkle with amusement. "Hazelnut is Ger's favorite."

"Mine, too," I challenge.

"Ooh, Hannah," Henry chides. "Do I detect a bit of snark?"

"Me?" I smile sweetly. "No, sir."

Henry's quiet laugh sends a jolt of goosebumps skittering down my arms, and my nipples tighten to little buds beneath my blouse. His bright blue eyes linger on mine. "I'll ask Pam to make sure we get two canisters of Hazelnut from now on."

"Good. And, thank you. That's nice of you." I've never seen the playful side of Henry Sloane. I kind of like it.

He sticks his hands into his pockets and rocks back on his heels. "I can be nice."

Gerald stifles a laugh with a series of coughs, and Henry's eyebrow ticks upward. He's exceptionally pleasant today. What gives?

"We'll see how nice you are after we drive by Sloane's on Fifth," Gerald quips. "If we're really going to do this, we need to hurry up. I'll have to make do without coffee."

"Everything okay?" I glance from Gerald to Sloane.

"It's all relative these days," Henry says. "Ever since that damn video took hold, there hasn't been a dull moment, that's for sure."

A pang of guilt niggles in my chest. Running a Fortune 500 must be stressful enough without a vocal group of activists trying to bring you down.

"It's about time we got you out of that office." Gerald's eyes light up with mischief. "We're off to scope out the protest on Fifth Avenue."

"A protest?" Oh fuck. Organized by Vi's group of friends, no doubt.

Gerald nods. "I was hunting for info on the video and came across intel on a protest. We're going to check it out."

Intel? Jesus. Gerald must think he's FBI all of a sudden. "Is that a good idea?" I ask.

"What could go wrong? We're just driving by." He wags his brows. "Incognito."

I glance at Henry. "Does your communications team know you're doing this? I can think of ten reasons off the top of my head why this is a bad idea."

"Like what?" Gerald's head cocks to the side, challenging me for trying to put a kibosh on his covert operation.

"Well, for starters, what if someone sees you? They'll expect you to make a statement. You won't be able to pretend you just happened to be driving by."

Henry shrugs. "I'll make Gerald say something."

With his hands out in front of him, Gerald takes a step back. "Oh, no, I don't think so. These women *hate* you. I've read all the nasty things they're saying about you online." He shakes his head. "I like my job, but I don't get paid enough to take a bullet for you."

My eyes roll skyward. "No one is getting shot. But you really should have something prepared to say, just in case. Please talk to your comms people before you bury yourself."

Gerald looks at Henry, and I sip my coffee while they contemplate my suggestion.

"Come with us," Henry blurts.

I choke on my drink and cough out, "Me?"

"Sure." He grabs a carrot muffin from the tray as he speaks, and I can't tell if he's being facetious. "You sound like you know what you're talking about. My communications team is too uptight to support this initiative."

I bite back my surprise at his blasé. They're not uptight— it's their job to protect the company image. This *initiative* could turn into a nightmare. "I really shouldn't. Kyle's in a meeting —"

"Don't worry about Kyle. I'll have Pam let him know you're with me for the rest of the day." He clears his throat. "With us."

***

On our way to the underground parking lot, I send Kyle a brief email from my phone to let him know the ads I've been working on are close to completion and that I'll send him designs to review in the morning. The last thing I want is for him to think I'm bailing on my work to go schmooze with the big boss. Although, that's exactly what I should be doing to try and get ahead.

When we emerge from the elevator, a slick black Mercedes

Benz is waiting for us, its driver standing beside the rear passenger door.

Henry leads us over to the older gentleman who must be ten years past retirement. "Afternoon, Frank. How are you?"

"I'm wonderful. It's a beautiful day to be alive," he says with genuine enthusiasm as he extends his hand to shake Henry's. "Yourself?"

"Same."

Frank laughs a hearty rumble that emanates from somewhere deep. "One day, you'll say that and mean it."

"Yeah, maybe. You know where we're headed?"

"Yes, sir. We're just waiting for Trent—oh, here he comes now." Frank gestures behind us and when I turn, I find a security guard booking it toward us.

Henry glances at Gerald, perplexed. "I thought we agreed it would just be us?"

"It never hurts to have backup," Gerald says, his expression equal parts sheepish and relieved.

Sloane shrugs. "Sure, what the hell. The more the merrier. We'll squish into the back and Trent can ride shotgun."

"Are you sure you don't want the limo, sir?" Frank asks.

"No. This is fine. We don't want to draw attention." Henry winks at me and grins.

I fight the urge to shake my head. He isn't taking this protest seriously. If he's not careful, he'll get himself in deeper shit. And why he's picked me to join him on this gong show is beyond me. Sure, I have the degree to back up any advice I give, but I don't have an ounce of real-life experience.

Frank opens the door of the fancy corporate car, and Henry motions for Gerald and me to get in. "After you."

Gerald ducks in first and I follow, scooting along the black leather with one hand on the back of my skirt to prevent flashing my panties. I buckle myself in as Sloane climbs in next to me.

With three of us on the seat, it's a little crowded but not uncomfortably so. Poor Gerald leans toward the window as if I have the plague, but Sloane has no qualms taking up his fair share of space. His thigh brushes mine, and my body temperature shoots up ten degrees.

Lord, it's hot in here.

I fight the urge to fan my face. There's no reason to get all worked up. I'm in the back of a car with Henry Sloane. So what? It's no big deal.

My body disagrees.

I zero in on where his thigh is touching my bare leg. Mmmmm. I've seen his rock-hard quads up close. Up really, *really* close when I zoomed in on the underwear ad that popped up on my laptop screen last night. It's not my fault those things keep following me around to taunt me. I only googled him once this week. Maybe twice. No naked pics of him exist online.

Sloane shifts on the seat, so our legs no longer touch, and it severs my wayward thoughts. My gaze snaps up to the passing street signs. We're still a few blocks away, yet the sidewalks are more visibly crowded, everyone seemingly heading in the same direction.

Henry turns to me, his eyes serious as if he's just clued in that this is not a game. "What should I say?" He points outside his window. "You know, worst-case scenario."

I could kiss that sweet pout of his. Finally, he gets it. "You say you're sorry. And try to sound like its genuine. It's basic issues management. Acknowledge the issue. Accept responsibility. Apologize."

Sloane hums as if contemplating everything I've said.

"For the record, there's also corrective action—but that means you'd say you're making changes to the clothing line to make it more consumer-friendly. But I guess you can just ignore that."

Henry meets my challenging stare, and for a moment, I think he might tell me off for being so candid.

But he doesn't.

"How do you know all this?" he asks, his tone soft.

"School." I shrug as if it's no big deal, but really, it is. I'm proud of how far I've come. I'm the first in my family to earn a degree. "I started out in graphic design, but I found the marketing and communications classes so fascinating I stayed a few extra years to get my Master's."

"Ah," he says. "That makes sense. Sounds like you're overqualified to work for Kyle."

"Maybe," I counter. "Everyone has to start somewhere. For me, that means a three-month contract at Evans, Roth and Sloane." I grin. "I figure that's long enough to prove myself. If not, I'll have three months of amazing work experience to add to my resume."

"You're determined, that's good."

I grin. "That, and stubborn."

***

Traffic slows to a crawl as we close in on Sloane's on Fifth, and my blood pressure skyrockets. It's not the coffee making me jittery. Outside the car, more and more people head in the direction of the store holding handmade cardboard signs. I scan the thick black headlines.

We are every woman.

Beauty comes in *every* size.

Exclusivity isn't sexy.

One of the signs bears a zoomed-in closeup of me from the video, and thank God my face is blurred. But imagine if it wasn't. My stomach launches itself into my throat. I need to find that money and pay Davis before he sends the video to Sloane.

"This is a bad idea," I mutter. Bad, bad, bad. "We need to go back."

Beside me, Gerald's leg bounces like a jackhammer he can't control. "She might be right, mate."

Henry's focus remains on what's happening beyond his window. "No. We're here."

The crowd that's gathered outside of Sloane's is more substantial than I imagined, and traffic is at a standstill. We're well and truly stuck in the heart of every PR person's worst nightmare. Police officers line the edge of the sidewalk, keeping protesters away from the road, but there are too many people and too few cops. Protesters spill out onto the street, creating a greater sense of chaos within the gridlock.

Next to us, a woman bends over and tries to peer inside the window of our car. Without thinking, I duck and hide—right into Henry's chest.

My palm meets solid abs, and time stands still as Sloane's familiar scent surrounds me. Oh, man, he smells good. Not just good but strong and manly, all-consuming panty-melting good. I lift my head and find him staring down at me.

"Sorry." I separate my body from his, but I can't tear my

gaze away.

His gentle smile has me silently swooning. "They can't see us," he says. "Tinted windows."

"I know. I didn't mean to do that."

"Shhhh." Gerald shushes us and cups his hand around his ear. "Do you hear that?" He points into the crowd then hits the button to crack his window. "She's making a speech. Blimey, these ladies mean business."

At the podium in front of Sloane's on Fifth, a young woman waves to get everyone's attention. "Henry Sloane is a bully," she yells into the microphone. "A big, corporate bully who thinks it's okay to market clothing that *every woman needs to be beautiful* while only designing clothes that fit one percent of the population. News flash, Sloane: Size matters." The crowd laughs before quickly quieting down. "It's time to stand up to bullies like Henry Sloane and let them know exclusivity isn't acceptable. Not anymore."

Everyone cheers, waving their signs high in the air as the woman continues her speech.

I glance at Henry to try and gauge what he's thinking. His brows pinch together as if he's deep in thought, and his jaw is set so firm I think his teeth might crack.

"I'm not a bully," he says, more to himself than me.

I pat his leg before pulling my hand away. "They just want to be heard," I tell him softly. "They want someone to listen."

Sloane inhales long and deep before exhaling. "I hear them," he says, so quiet it's hard to make out his words.

Before I realize what's happening, Henry unbuckles his seatbelt and swings his door wide open. He disappears into the crowd, and I watch in awe as he's swallowed up by the masses.

Trent jumps out next, leaving his door ajar in his haste as he follows in Henry's wake.

I turn to Gerald. "What the fuck just happened?"

He shrugs. "Henry Sloane may be a ruthless businessman—but he's no bully."

CHAPTER
five

Henry Sloane is a fucking genius.

And he's equally stupid.

In the span of ten minutes, he's turned hundreds of protesting women into his new fan base. But he's also promised them the world—a new line of women's clothing in three times as many sizes as he offers now. All to launch in sixty days at a public fashion show on the first of July.

Two months. Jesus. What the hell is he thinking?

Trent and Henry emerge from the horde of people like two divers resurfacing from shark-infested water. They quickly climb into the car before Frank can even unlatch his seatbelt. Sloane slides back in beside me, grinning like an idiot. "See? They love me. No need to bring PR into this."

"Yeah, they love you all right," I deadpan. "Until they find out you can't deliver what you promised."

"We'll make it happen," he says with overflowing confidence that rivals my doubt.

"How is that even possible?" I challenge. "How long did it take your team to design the first women's line?"

He shrugs. "About a year, maybe a little less. I wasn't heavily involved." Henry's brows draw together as silence fills the car. His eyes flicker with understanding before he frowns. "Shit. I see what you're getting at."

Gerald chuckles, seemingly amused by Henry's plight. "You've buried yourself, mate."

Sloane hums a questionable sound. "No. I've got it." He shifts on the seat to face Gerald and me, and smiles. "What if it's just a pilot available only at Sloane's on Fifth. Exclusive to the 212."

"A Manhattan exclusive? I like it," Gerald says. "Two-one-two—like the area code."

Henry points a finger at Gerald. "Exactly. We're taking the designs we already have and tweaking them to make them bigger. That will save a lot of time. If it's a success, we'll roll it out to all the other stores."

I nod. Damn, he's good. "That might just work."

"There's only one problem," Gerald says. "What about Bastien? If he's not available, we're fucked." He glances at me, adding, "Bastien's the fashion designer we hired for the first project. Can't say I'm looking forward to working with that little bald-headed prick again. He was a giant pain in my arse."

Henry mutters a curse and leans forward to tap the edge of the front seat. "Back to the office, please, Frank. We've got no time to waste."

***

For the next twenty minutes, Sloane throws out ideas about the new line he's dubbed 212, while Gerald complains about his previous run-ins with Bastien. It continues in the elevator as we ride up to the fifty-second floor. I'm already sick of Bastien, and I haven't even met the guy.

"Why do you keep hiring him if he's such a jerk to work with?" I ask. "There are hundreds of designers for hire. This *is* New York, you know."

Gerald shakes his head. "None like Bastien. He's a connoisseur of fashion. Makes the impossible possible. He's a jerk because he *can* be. He knows he's irreplaceable."

I scoff. "Well, he must be *very good* if he's made you believe he's the only one who can do his job."

The corner of Henry's mouth turns up, and Gerald scowls back at him. "What are you smiling about? You said yourself that he's a bloody genius."

"I've also called him a twat on more than one occasion. No one is irreplaceable, Ger. It would serve you well to remember that."

The elevator doors open before Gerald can respond, and a young woman stalks toward us, her heels click-clacking obnoxiously on the floor. Even from twenty feet away, I can tell that she's not one to mess with. Her fitted black suit hugs her willowy twenty-something body, and her jet-black hair is pulled away from her face. If it weren't for her sour demeanor, she'd be quite pretty.

"Oh, here we go," Gerald mutters.

We file out of the elevator just as she reaches us. "There you are, Henry. Come with me. I need to speak with you urgently."

Henry's expression hardens as he sets his steely gaze on her.

"Eleanor, hello. How are you? Keeping busy? How's *Travis?*"

Her resting bitch face stiffens. "Don't start with me. This is important."

"No." He grits his teeth. "It's not. Call Pam and schedule an appointment like everyone else."

She huffs like a spoiled teen but refrains from stomping her foot. "You really screwed up this time. You know better than to show up at a protest. You're already trending on Twitter. And you'll be all over the news by tonight. A journalist from the New York Times called within ten minutes of your speech. They want details on this new, *expanded product line,*" she says, adding air quotes to the last few words.

Sloane's one-sided shrug is as uncommitted as I am to my diet. "Don't care. They can call Pam—same as you."

Eleanor crosses her arms over her chest and tips her head to one side as if that will help prove her point. "You oversold yourself, and you know it. I've already talked to PR. We've all agreed—you have to issue a retraction."

"No."

"Henry," she fumes.

Ignoring her, Sloane turns to Gerald. "Can you find Bastien's previous contract and revise it? Bring it to my office when it's ready, and I'll see if Pam can get in touch with him."

Sloane rests his palm on the curve of my back. "Do you have a minute to see me in my office?"

I glance up at him and pray the heat creeping up my chest hasn't had a chance to reach my face. "I do. My afternoon got cleared this morning." By him.

His expression softens. "That's right. Let's go." He turns to Eleanor as we leave. "I'll tell Pam to watch for your call."

Guiding us away from Eleanor, we walk toward his office. When we round the corner, he drops his hand from my back and sighs. "I'm sorry. I hope that didn't make you uncomfortable."

"It didn't." His hand on my back was a welcome addition to my day. But Eleanor? She's a bitch I could have lived without.

Sloane stops at Pam's desk and leaves her with strict instructions to get ahold of Bastien. Regardless of where he might be in the world, Henry wants him here pronto.

Inside his office, Henry veers to the right and stops in front of a small bar that's built into the side of the wall. He holds up a decanter of amber liquid. "Scotch?"

"Oh, no, thank you. I don't drink."

"Not at all?" he questions.

"Not often. It tends to get me into trouble," I tell him, smiling.

"Me, too." He grins. "But I don't let that stop me. It helps me think." After setting several cubes of ice inside a crystal glass, he adds three fingers of scotch and takes a sip. "God, I needed that," he sighs.

Sloane takes another drink, eying me over the top of his glass.

Under his watchful gaze, I become hyper-aware of my body, picking at fuzz that isn't there and smoothing non-existent wrinkles on my skirt. I clasp my hands in front of me to keep them from fidgeting. "What did you want to see me for?"

He laughs to himself, but it sounds more like a scoff. "Nothing, really. I just needed an excuse to get away from Eleanor." Henry gestures to one of the leather chairs. "But now that you're here, I think I'll pick your brain."

"Okay, but I'm not sure how much help I'll be." I sit where

he suggests, and he takes the other chair that's angled toward me. In this position, our legs are close but not quite touching.

After a quiet pause, he says, "So, you're a woman…"

"Yes. Last time I checked," I deadpan, fighting my smile.

He chokes on his scotch and laughs. "I deserved that. It's been a weird day. I'm off my game."

I grin. "I'm just giving you a hard time."

"I see that." His gaze travels over me, lingering on where our knees are almost touching, and he takes another sip of scotch. "The other day, you mentioned how some women might have trouble fitting the clothes Bastien designed. Can you elaborate?"

Heat floods my cheeks without warning, and my fingers play at the hem of my skirt.

"I'm sorry if this is too personal," he blurts. "I'm trying to get a better idea of where we went wrong. I don't want to make the same mistakes on 212."

I draw a breath. "Okay, um…there are several things." My hand waves circles involuntarily in front of my chest as I try to choose my words carefully. Boobs, breasts, chest? There's no good option.

"Just tell me how it is. Don't sugar coat it. I appreciate how candid you've been with me."

Nodding, I tell him, "Okay. Well, let's start above the belt."

Sloane downs the rest of his drink and his tongue sneaks out to lick the bead of scotch from his lip. "Okay. Above the belt."

"And I want to caveat this by saying that all women are built differently. What fits me won't fit the next person."

He nods. "Note taken."

"Personally, I often have trouble with shirts. Blouses, in

particular." As if riveted by our conversation, he leans in close as I gesture to my breasts. "I have, um… My breasts are… There's not always enough room in this area," I tell him. "Don't get me wrong," I add. "Your bras are great. I tried on a pretty teal one once, and it fit perfectly."

"But you didn't buy it?" His brow crinkles with genuine concern.

I shake my head. "It was lovely… but out of my price range," I tell him, glancing at my borrowed shoes.

"I understand. This is all good, Hannah. Thank you." Henry stands from his chair and fills up his glass with more scotch. "What about below the belt? Any concerns there?"

"Oh, I didn't have time to try on the matching panties," I tell him, surprised at how easily the word slips off my tongue.

Sloane closes his eyes for a moment before looking back at me. "I mean with skirts or pants, that sort of thing."

My eyes grow wide, and heat creeps back up my neck. I wring my fingers in my lap. "Of course. Uhh, well, sometimes jeans get that gap in the back," I stammer. "If you could solve that, you're guaranteed to be a millionaire." I cringe. He's already a millionaire, genius. I shake my head as if that will take me back in time. "Sorry."

"Don't apologize. I know what you mean."

"Lots of women get the gap. It's a thing. I don't know what else to say, I'm not a fashion designer. I'm just a girl who has a hard time finding clothes to fit her. But that's the story of every woman's life. I'm really no different."

"Don't discount yourself so easily. This is very helpful. I had no idea shopping for clothes was anything but fun."

I blow out a puff of air. "I wish. I mean, sometimes it *can* be fun. Nothing beats finding the perfect outfit. It's exhilarating. But on the flip side, imagine going into a store and finding out nothing will fit you." I wrinkle my nose. "It sucks. And it feeds into every insecurity and makes you crazy. You swear off breakfast, lunch and dinner for the foreseeable future and you promise yourself that you'll get up early and hit the gym." I laugh to myself. God, how many times have I done just that? The snooze button has more power than my will.

Sloane stares at me, seemingly mesmerized as he mutters a dumbfounded, "Huh."

"It's true," I continue. "It doesn't matter how thin or fit you are, there'll always be something—a sore spot—that's super sensitive and sits close to the surface. One small poke is all it takes to deflate years of built-up confidence. For some, that might be as simple as trying on a blouse that won't button up."

"Like our friend in the video." Sloane sits back down in the chair, and his leg brushes mine.

I nod. "Yes, exactly. Maybe she was having a bad day, and that blouse just poked her sore spot. *Maybe* she had no idea her rant would end up online."

Sloane hums as if considering that option. "It's possible. It certainly doesn't paint her in a good light."

"That video is humiliating." It plagues my mind every waking hour. Even more, now that Davis is breathing down my neck. "Are you still trying to track her down?" I ask.

He shakes his head. "I don't think it matters anymore. The damage is done. Expanding the line is my only option to save face."

"Really?" I sigh. "That's a terrible reason. If you don't want to expand it, issue a retraction like Eleanor suggested."

He scoffs. "She would love that." Sloane downs the rest of his drink and swirls the ice around in the bottom of his glass. "I'm not opposed to expanding the line. I'm more pissed at myself for not standing my ground from the beginning. I never wanted to add a portfolio for women's clothing." He swirls the ice again. "I made my bed. I'll lie in it."

Forcing my brain to avoid the rabbit hole that leads to Sloane naked in his bed, I focus on the meaning behind his words. "You wanted to stick with what you knew—men's clothing."

"Yes. And I didn't want to deal with Eleanor—for obvious reasons."

Because she's a bitch? Because the two of them dated? Fucked? The reasons aren't all that obvious to me.

Henry brings his glass to his lips and crunches on an ice cube. "Another stupid decision on my part. Isn't that the first lesson they teach you in business school? Don't sleep with your subordinates?"

Okay, so they fucked, big deal. I'm not jealous. "Sounds like a good rule," I lie. It's a terrible rule. And it squashes every one of my fantasies.

"It's been several years, but I still can't take her advice seriously. As the Director of Fashion, she has a heavy influence over several of my teams. PR and comms included. Makes it hard to tell if their advice is in my best interest or hers. Sometimes it feels like the world is waiting for me to fail. When I do, you can bet Eleanor will be waiting in the wings to rub it in." Henry's expression softens as he studies me. "I'm sorry. I don't know why I'm telling you this. I blame the scotch."

His honesty tugs at my heart. I'd never imagined a man like

Sloane to have a vulnerable side, but it's clear from his dejected expression that he's let his guard down. Underneath that stellar body and inside that sharp business mind of his, is a man with insecurities just like the rest of us. It's endearing.

Resting my hand on his forearm, I meet his gaze. "For what it's worth, I don't think you'll fail. All you need is the right people beside you... and some extra money to throw at the project to speed up the timelines." I inject my voice with confidence. "If anyone can pull this off, it's you."

His head bobs a single, deliberate nod, and slowly, his frown morphs into an expression I know well.

Determination.

Only, the problem with determination is that it can consume you. It can cloud your head and make you do crazy things until the line between determination and desperation is indistinguishable.

Sloane jumps from his chair and rushes to his desk. "You're spot on, Hannah," he says, picking up the phone. "Pam, please clear my calendar for tomorrow morning. Also, block off Boardroom Three until noon." He pauses. "I don't care if Doug has it booked. Bump him. He can reschedule."

Even from across the room, I can make out the conviction blazing in his eyes. Whatever he's decided, he's on a mission.

Henry hangs up the phone and walks back to where I'm sitting. "I *do* have the right people." He plops down in the chair beside me and grins. "Because starting tomorrow, you report to me."

CHAPTER *six*

The following morning at five to nine, I find myself back in Boardroom Three. This time, by invitation—not bad luck.

At the oblong table, five of us sit curved around one end, with Sloane at the head and Eleanor and Pam on either side of him.

Bastien, a bald man in red, thick-rimmed glasses, sits across from me, staring daggers at Sloane. "I postponed my flight to Paris for this," he says, a French accent lacing his words. "Renée is not happy with me. She hates to travel alone."

"I'm sure you can find a way to make it up to her. You're creative," Sloane says. "Did you have a chance to read over the contract?"

"I did. Your timeline is very tight. We can negotiate my rate later in private."

"I believe the offer is quite generous."

Bastien puckers his lips. "Perhaps. But I've since been enlightened. Now, I think it warrants renegotiation."

Sloane glances at Eleanor, and she immediately looks away. Guilty. I bet she gave Bastien some inside information before our meeting. That's sneaky. Now I understand Sloane's reluctance in trusting her advice.

If Henry's upset at Eleanor's betrayal, he doesn't show it. "If it's beyond your skill level, I completely understand. There are plenty of other designers I could hire. This is New York, you know," he says, parroting my words.

Visibly outraged, Bastien squares his shoulders and pushes his bright-red glasses up the bridge of his nose. "Fous le camp! I didn't say I *couldn't* do it."

It's been ten years since I took French, but I'm pretty sure Bastien just gave Sloane a big fuck you.

A slur of French spills from Henry's mouth and Bastien battles back, slamming his fist on the table. My gaze bounces from man to man, trying but failing to follow their foreign argument. Who knew Angry Henry could get any sexier? He can yell at me anytime he wants, as long as it's in French.

"Gentelman, calmez-vous," Eleanor rests her palm on Bastien's forearm. "If you have concerns, Bastien, please tell us."

"I do have concerns," he says. "Many."

"Fine." Henry opens a leather-bound notebook and aims his pen at the paper. "Let's hear them."

"The timeline is near impossible."

"Near impossible, but not," Henry counters. "We'll hire more people to help you."

Bastien's lips press together as he draws a deep breath in

through his nose like a bull ready to charge. Good Lord, he's dramatic. "Every design will need altering."

"Well, sure. That's a given," Sloane deadpans, making another note. "What else?"

"I need a fit model—a live mannequin for our baseline."

"That's easy. You have contacts."

Bastien shakes his head. "The only ones I know are très petites. I need someone with—" he hums "—How can I say this nicely? More meat."

I fight the urge to roll my eyes. More meat? All he needs is someone who eats breakfast, lunch and dinner. Or, I don't know, anyone who's not a skeleton.

A quiet knock interrupts our meeting. The boardroom door cracks open, and Kyle pokes his head in, gesturing with his hand for me to come closer.

Excusing myself from the table, I make my way over.

"Sorry," he whispers when I reach him. "I'm meeting with the DC Group at noon, and I'm not sure the status of their file."

"It's done," I tell him. "I updated it based on the feedback that was listed in the notes. Printed copies are in a blue folder on my desk. I was going to drop them off to you after this meeting."

"Ah," he sighs. "Thank you. You're a lifesaver. I wasn't sure if you'd had a chance to get to it before Henry stole you away." He grins. "Congrats, by the way."

"Thanks."

"I'll let you get back," he says, pulling the door closed behind him.

When I return to my seat, everyone is quiet, watching me intently.

"How tall are you, Hannah?" Sloane asks, breaking the silence.

"Pardon?" What's that have to do with anything?

"Five-six?" He guesses.

I sit back in my chair. "Five-seven. Why?"

Henry peers at Bastien. "Well?"

Bastien hums. "A little short." He stares at me, his head tipping to one side and then the other.

Jeez. I half expect him to hold his hands out in front of him and frame me between his thumb and forefingers.

Like a model.

A model...

Oh shit.

"No. No, no, no." My hands tremble in my lap as I glance nervously at Sloane. "Whatever you're thinking, back that train up."

"I can make it work," Bastien says, nodding.

The smile that splits Henry's face would melt my panties if it weren't tainted by its meaning.

"Please don't. I'm not a model. Nothing ever fits me. I have curves, and my waist is too small for my hips. I'm the worst person to use as a baseline." Clamping my jaw shut, I stop ten more excuses from tumbling out.

"We need a starting point, and you'll do until we can hire others." Bastien stands from his chair and reaches across the table to shake Sloane's hand before turning back to me. "We start tomorrow. My studio. Six-thirty."

"Wait. Let's talk about this," I sputter.

"Someone will get you the details." Bastien waves to the rest of us. "Au revoir."

Without another word, Bastien leaves, and Pam follows behind him before I can even stand from the table. At this point, I'm not sure I could get up if I wanted to. A model. Me? Jesus. "You're crazy," I tell Sloane.

"She's right." Eleanor closes the boardroom door, shutting Sloane and me inside with her. "I don't know why you're doing this, Henry. You're a fool." She glances at me, but it's closer to a sneer. "We're not in the business of making clothes for fat people."

I suck in an audible breath. I can't believe she said that.

"*We* are not in the business of anything," Sloane growls. "This isn't Evans, Roth and Eleanor."

She huffs. "Since when did you lower your standards? Why are you caving to the pressure of these people? So they can't fit in the clothes—tough shit. Go on a diet, Fatty."

Pushing away from the table, I stand and grab my notepad. "Are you for real?"

"What? Did I offend you, Hannah?" Her eyes twinkle with mirth. If she's trying to piss me off, she's doing a damn good job.

"No, you didn't offend me." I glance at Sloane to gauge his reaction. Judging from his curious expression, he doesn't appear to have any issue with me speaking up. "You're right. The current line of clothes doesn't fit me. And I could probably lose a few pounds, but I'm an eight. Sometimes a ten." I shake my head. "That's not that big. You're pretty narrow-minded if you think a business model with a larger size range won't broaden the market—and the profits, for that matter."

"Sloane's brand is too high-end to have chunky women trying to squeeze their over-sized asses into Bastien's designs."

I ball my fists at my side. "A ten isn't fat!"

"Maybe not to you."

I bite my lip to keep from calling her a bitch. It's no use arguing with ignorance, but I can't help it. "And how can you talk about people like that? As a woman, you should have more respect. We all come in different sizes. That doesn't make one customer more entitled to wear the clothes than another."

"I'm sorry that you're double digits, honey. Lay off the donuts, and maybe one day you'll get rid of that muffin top." Eleanor crinkles her nose. "I bet your jeans get that gap at the back, don't they?" She pouts her lips in a faux sad face. "You poor thing. I've never had that problem. Then again, *I'm a two.*"

"Enough, Eleanor!" Sloane points at the door. "Unless you want off this project, I suggest you keep your opinion to yourself. Nobody wants to hear it. Including me."

"You're making a mistake, Henry. This whole 212 idea is flawed." Eleanor takes a step toward him and reaches for his arm, but he's having none of it.

"Get out."

"But—"

He waves his finger toward the door again. "Out!"

Huffing, she turns on her heel and slams the door closed behind her.

"I should go, too," I say, reaching for the doorknob. "I've got a couple of things I need to get to Kyle." I also need time to recover from the assault of Eleanor's words.

"Wait." The sincerity in Henry's voice gives me pause.

Without looking back, I wait for him to continue. The adrenaline of arguing with Eleanor is fading, and shame quickly takes its place. She's poked my sore spot. Worse, she's gouged it open in front of a beautiful man who would never understand. There'll always be people smaller than me. And people bigger. My value isn't determined by my size. Logically, I get that. But my heart, the emotional part of me won't ever believe it.

"This shouldn't warrant saying, but you are *not* fat, not in the slightest. I want you to disregard everything Eleanor just said. She was way out of line."

I nod, but it's too late. The damage is done. I stare at the frosted glass, focusing on the shadowy figures of people walking by.

"Hannah?"

I close my eyes. Make me disappear.

Henry's masculine scent finds its way to my nose before the heat of his hand finds my shoulder. "Look at me." He nudges my shoulder until I turn to face him, my back to the boardroom door.

Swallowing my pride, I lift my gaze to meet his.

"If you don't want to do this, you don't have to," he says. "Someone else can be the live model. I'll find something else for you to do that doesn't involve taking your clothes off." He half-smiles at his joke.

Dropping my gaze, I contemplate my options. Working with Bastien will place me way outside my comfort zone. Way, way, outside. But I'd also be helping Sloane at a time when he needs it. It could be another stepping stone to full-time employment. It's the move that's better for my career but suicide for my self-esteem.

He tips my chin up, and my eyes follow, locking onto his beautiful blues. Why's he have to be so goddamn pretty?

"Say something," he whispers.

"I'll do it," I say, injecting my voice with confidence. "But I can't promise I won't butt heads with Eleanor."

His features relax as he smiles. "Thank you. I could kiss you." His eyes jut wide. "But I won't," he stammers. "That would be inappropriate."

I stare at his lips as they part. "Yes. You have rules."

His smile falters as he nods. "Yeah. Rules."

***

Bastien's studio is in the heart of the Meat Packing District and from the outside, it looks like a dump. Pieces of red brick crumble from beneath the warehouse-style windows, and the steel door entrance could use another coat of paint. But from the inside, wow, it takes my breath away.

Trista, a slender woman in high-waisted shorts and a fitted blouse, leads me through the studio, her clipboard hugged tight to her chest. She gestures to a closed door on her left. "Bastien's office."

I nod.

"Ladies' room," she adds, pointing to her right. "Everything else is this way."

We pass through a large doorway and the height of the room doubles, extending up two stories. At first glance, it looks like chaos, but upon closer inspection, it's clear the space is meant to adapt to multiple uses. Wall dividers break up the room into various areas that house racks of clothing, lighting, props, and even cameras.

On the far side of the room, Bastien directs a worker to move a big, round platform to the area in front of a curved bank of mirrors.

"Ahh, good," he says, coming over to us. "There you are. If

we're going to do this, it gets done right. Understand?"

"Yes."

"Good. As you can appreciate, the timeline is very tight. There is no modesty in here. You walk through that door, you're a human mannequin, okay? You'll be poked and prodded, measured and remeasured. You suck it up, oui?"

"Sounds fun," I say, sarcastically as two men wheel a rack of lingerie past us.

"My style, my methods are unconventional. More importantly, they are proprietary. What happens in this studio stays here. Understand?"

I nod.

"Let me hear it."

"I understand. What happens here stays here. I'm good with that, Bastien. You're going to see me almost naked. That stays here."

"Good." Bastien leads me toward the bank of mirrors. "Let's get started, shall we? Take off your clothes and step onto the podium."

I peer around. "Right here? In front of everyone?"

He groans. "Hannah, what did I say about modesty?"

"I know, I know. I get it," I sigh. "Just this once, could we ease into it? Please? I'm not used to this."

Bastien rolls his eyes and sighs. "Fine. Trista, take Hannah to the dressing area."

"Yes, sir." Trista taps my arm, and I follow her to another area with a row of fitting rooms that line one wall. "There's a robe in there that you can wear," she says, pushing one of the doors open.

"Thank you." Inside the spacious stall, I strip down to my

bra and panties and head back to the podium in the robe. I've already pissed Bastien off with my request, I don't need him bitching about me taking too long to change.

With the fluffy belt tied tight around my waist, I step onto the foot-high platform. My reflection stares back at me from three different angles. Ugh. Under the bright white light, every freckle, every flaw, every imperfection is on display for a room full of strangers. I tuck my long blonde hair behind my ear.

Deep breath.

I can do this.

This is about more than just me.

This is about girls with curves, women who ought to celebrate their shape.

This is for the ninety-nine percent.

"Any time now." Bastien stalks closer, a tape measure draped around his neck.

"All right." I draw a calming breath. "Okay, I'm ready." My fingers play at the knot on the robe, and I watch in the mirror as it parts to reveal the white lace bra and matching panties I picked out this morning.

It's now or never, but never is not an option.

Closing my eyes, I drop my shoulders and shrug off the robe into the waiting arms of one of Bastien's staff. There. The hard part is over.

"Très bien." Bastien peeks around me. "Oh, hello. I didn't think you were coming."

"I changed my mind."

The deep, familiar voice sends goosebumps skittering down my arms.

My gaze snaps to the mirror, locking onto bright, blue eyes.

I suck in a breath.
Sloane.

CHAPTER *seven*

I want to crawl into a hole and die.

Scratch that.

I want Sloane to crawl into a hole and die.

He's a bastard. Showing up at Bastien's studio, knowing I'd be on display like this, practically naked while he gets to gawk at me from the sideline and examine my every flaw.

If he's disgusted by my body, he hides it well. His expression remains all business as he steps closer, shaking Bastien's hand before smiling at me. "Good morning, Hannah."

I force a tight-lipped smile and watch in the mirror as blotchy red patches climb my neck. My cheeks flush as if I've caught an instant fever. Wringing my fingers, I try to stop them from shaking. My body vibrates—either from pent up anger at Sloane's appearance or from not having eaten a proper meal since my run-in with Eleanor. It doesn't matter which.

Bastien moves around my body, directing me to raise my arms then lower them as he measures my bust. "This won't do," he grumbles. "Ugh. Trista, get her into a decent bra. Thirty-four C," he announces to the room.

"Yes, sir." She extends her hand, and I take it, stepping off the platform. What little confidence I had has now deflated. Trista hands me back the robe, and I slip it on, grateful for the reprieve.

"Sorry," she whispers, once we're out of earshot. "I know Bastien seems like a jerk. His standards are very high, but that's why he's so good."

That's what Gerald said, too. "It's fine. I get it. This was the nicest bra I had." When we reach a rack of lingerie, I ask her, "Does Henry Sloane come here often?"

Confirming my suspicion, she shakes her head. "Never. At least not lately. Unfortunately, I didn't work for Bastien when Henry was modeling. I've only ever worked with Eleanor."

A quiet scoff sneaks past my lips before I can stop it. Trista's gaze snaps to mine. "Not a fan?"

I shake my head.

"Me neither." She leans in close. "I heard she just got fired —is that true?"

"Fired? No way. I was just in a meeting with her yesterday." Although, it's possible, now that I think of it, Sloane was pretty pissed with her after what she said.

"So, technically not fired," she clarifies. "Bastien said she's going to be working for another arm of the company now. Like a promotion, but not by choice. Apparently, Sloane couldn't stand to look at her anymore. He called it a *win-win*. She must have really pissed him off."

"No kidding." My body buzzes with excitement. If Eleanor's gone, that works for me. There's no love lost between us.

Trista holds up a lace bra that I recognize from Sloane's on Fifth. "You have a color preference? Black? Purple?"

"They're all beautiful."

"Get her the teal one."

Trista and I whip around to find Sloane hovering behind us. My pulse skyrockets. I hope he didn't hear us talking about Eleanor.

He points to some bras on the rack nearby. "The lace one. Panties, too." Henry smiles at me. "That's the one, isn't it?"

I nod, my face heating for the second time this morning. *He remembered.* I attempt to shake off the fluttering sensation in my belly, but give up trying. Even if he's only doing it to be nice, it's still sweet.

"Don't take too long." Henry's faux grimace makes me grin. "Bastien is not a patient man."

Trista laughs. "That's an understatement."

Sloane leaves and Trista fans her face, eyes wide in awe. "I don't normally swoon, but OMG, he's dreamy. And funny, too. I wasn't expecting that."

"Yeah, he's all right," I lie, grabbing the teal bra and panties in my size. "He's right, though. I'd better get changed before Bastien loses his shit."

***

For the next three hours, I try on outfit after outfit from Sloane's existing line. Using the size sixes as a starting point, Bastien examines each article to see how it hangs and makes notes on where the cut needs to change to make larger sizes.

More mortifying than trying on clothes I know won't fit, is Bastien's surprise when they don't.

I step into a black skirt and slide it up over my hips.

"Hallelujah! It fits. I can't believe it," Bastien shouts.

"I haven't done it up," I tell him quietly.

"I knew something would fit those hips," he continues. "It looks fabulous."

"I haven't done it up," I repeat, glancing at Henry, and hoping he's still busy on his phone.

He's not.

That phone's been pressed against his ear all morning, but of course, *now* he's done making calls.

Bastien cups his hand around his ear. "It's not zipped up? Ah, tabernac."

"Nothing is going to fit," I choke. "Just accept it." *I have.*

Ignoring me, he hands me a familiar white blouse, and my face grows red again. I slip it over my shoulders but don't bother trying to do it up. There's video proof that it barely buttons, but I can't tell a soul.

Bastien tugs the fabric together and fastens several of the buttons. "Whoo," he says. "This one's a little racy. You know who you look like? The girl in the video. Eh, Henry? You know who I'm talking about." He raises his pitch to a squeaky level. "Sloane can kiss my ass if he thinks I'll buy his over-priced scraps of fabric," Bastien paraphrases, laughing. "Poor girl looked like a high-end whore."

His mockery is more than I can handle, and my throat clogs with unshed tears. "I need a break."

"Not yet. I'm not done," Bastien says, still grinning.

Looking away, I clench my jaw and close my eyes. I can't

do this. The digs keep coming, one after the other. I'm done.

"Give her a break, Bastien, Jesus." I hear Sloane shuffling closer before his hand grips my wrist.

Twisting out of his hold, I step off the platform and make a beeline toward the changing room.

Inside the stall, I unfasten the buttons of the blouse so I can breathe and kick off the too-small skirt.

Stupid outfit.

I hang my head and let my tears wreak havoc on my mascara. I don't care. It's no secret that I'm in over my head here. My sympathy for women in the modeling business grows exponentially. It's no wonder they skip meals to maintain their willowy figures. I wouldn't wish this humiliation on my worst enemy.

Someone knocks on the door, but I ignore it.

"Hannah."

I sigh. Of course, it's him.

"Hannah, open up."

"I'm fine, Sloane."

"Are we on a last name basis now, O'Keefe? Sorry, I didn't realize."

Whoops.

"Open up. I want to talk to you. It's important. Are you decent?"

"I'm not naked," I say, wryly. "What is it?"

The door handle rattles before the door cracks open.

Glancing in the mirror, I quickly wipe my fingers under my eyes. Surprisingly, the damage looks more smokey than raccoon. At least one thing is going right for me today.

I back away from the door and cross my arms over my chest

—nothing new to see here.

"I'm sorry, I know this is probably hard for you," he says gently. "I understand if you want to call the whole thing off."

I have to give him props; his eyes remain above my neckline. Granted, I can't blame him. He's probably seen enough of me to last a lifetime. "I'm fine. I just need a minute."

Sloane steps into the stall and closes the door behind him. It's a good-sized fitting room, but with him in here, it feels as though it's shrunk to half the size.

"Don't lie to me."

"You're right. It's hard, okay?" Dropping my arms to my side, I poke at the discarded clothes on the floor with my toe. "That outfit looked ridiculous. *I* look ridiculous, even in pretty lingerie."

Sloane shakes his head. "That's not what I see. Not even close." With a hand on each of my shoulders, he turns me to face the mirror. "Tell me what you see."

I stare at my reflection. "God, where do I start? It's all bad."

He moves closer until he's flush against my back, heat from his body radiating against my exposed skin. "Be specific, Hannah."

Sloane's fingers graze my neck, and I watch in the mirror as he brushes my long, blonde hair back over my shoulders. He's not giving me the chance to hide, not even behind my hair.

Drawing a deep breath, I let him have the truth. "I hate my body. There're so many flaws. My breasts only look like this because of this fancy bra. They aren't that rounded at the top." I poke at my stomach. "It's not as toned as it could be. It's a little bit soft. I have too many curves. It doesn't matter how much weight I lose, they'll always be too big for my waist." I peer down at my legs. "My thighs touch. I hate that."

When Sloane says nothing, I force my eyes to meet his.

He sighs.

"You don't see it?" I ask, perplexed that he could be so oblivious. Bastien sees it. Eleanor sees it. *Everyone* sees it.

"I don't see it, Hannah."

Impossible.

Henry meets my gaze through the mirror. "I only see an astoundingly beautiful woman who's way too critical of herself."

"No." Clearly, he needs a new optician.

"I'll show you," he whispers, his breath tickling the shell of my ear. "Look."

In the dressing room stall, Sloane lifts his hand and gently cups my cheek. "I see soft, smooth skin, the delicate sprinkling of freckles on your face, your neck. The inside of your thigh." His hand skims down my torso, and I suck in a quiet breath. "Where you see too many curves, I see an hourglass figure, hips a man can grab onto when he fucks her, an ass he can dig his fingers into when she's bucking wild on top of him." Sloane wets his lips, and there's no mistaking the intentional swipe of his thumb over the swell of my breasts. "I look at you, and I can't help but wonder if your tight little buds are a soft, sweet pink to match your lips or something else entirely."

"Oh god," I breathe, my head lolling back against his shoulder.

Accepting my silent invitation, Henry kisses the sensitive spot beneath my ear and hums against my skin. "You're beautiful, Hannah."

Warmth pools between my legs and my knees threaten to

give, but Sloane's got it under control. He spins me around, pinning my back to the mirror. I buck forward to avoid the chill, but it's no use. His broad chest holds me in place. His lips a breadth away from mine.

He pulls back, his eyes alight with restraint yet questioning. Could he want this as much as I do?

"More," I tell him, the word coming out as a whisper. My fingers find his hair, and I crush his mouth to mine. If I'm dreaming, I don't ever want to wake.

A husky noise rumbles in his chest, and I match it with a whimper as our tongues dance with urgency.

I'm kissing Henry Sloane.

Henry Sloane is kissing *me*.

"Hannah?"

My body stiffens at the sound of my name.

Sloane breaks our kiss and places a finger over his lips as we stare wide-eyed at each other, quietly panting.

"I've got another outfit for you," Trista calls out from beyond the changing room. "Whenever you're ready. Bastien is eager to keep going."

"Okay," I choke out. "Thanks."

"Here you go." Two pieces of fabric appear over the top of the door. Her footsteps shuffle away before pausing. "Are you okay, Hannah? I know this is all new to you. It can be incredibly intimidating."

I clear my throat. "I just needed a break. I'm good now. Give me a sec, and I'll be right out."

"All right. Tell me if you need another break, and I'll make sure it happens."

"Thanks, Trista."

When the coast is clear, Sloane buries his face in my shoulder and kisses it gently. "I shouldn't be kissing you," he says against my skin. "I should know better than this."

"It's okay. I liked it." A lot. Way too much to admit.

He nods as he separates our bodies. "I'll let you get changed. You'd better get back before Bastien comes looking for you."

As quickly as he arrived, Sloane disappears from the changing room, and I'm left scrutinizing every detail of what just happened. I witnessed the softer side of Sloane, and it was glorious. I want to etch every sweet word he said to memory, but the way he left at the end leaves a niggling ache in my chest.

Back on Bastien's podium, I glance around the studio searching for Sloane.

"He's gone," Trista says answering my question before I can ask. "Said he had a meeting to get to."

My heart ricochets against my rib cage.

Or maybe, he's full of regret.

CHAPTER *eight*

Sloane panicked.

That's the only explanation my heart will entertain.

After a hellishly long day, I leave Bastien's studio somewhat deflated and walk the three-and-a-half miles home. The more I think about it, the more I'm convinced that Henry's kiss wasn't a pity prize for my tears. He wanted it. I'd felt his heart racing through his dress shirt, and more importantly, the bulge in his pants that may or may not have been his wallet.

I like him. And I've come to terms with the fact that a woman like me has nothing to entice a man like him. I have no money, no land, no noble title to offer him.

Despite all that, there's no denying the chemistry we exchanged in the fitting room. That man can kiss. And, he certainly didn't seem put off by my curves. My body trembles at the memory. By the time I reach my apartment, I'm re-energized. *I might stand a shot with Henry Sloane.*

Kicking my shoes off onto the mat beside the door, I announce, "I kissed *Henry Sloane!*" I'd rather scream it off the rooftops, but I have more restraint than that—just barely.

Vi and Tessa scramble off the couch, their lips swollen from making out. "Oh my God!" Tessa screeches, wiping smeared lipstick off her mouth. "Are you serious?"

I nod. This is too juicy to not share with my best friends.

"Yeah, right? You're messing with us," Vi adds, unconvinced.

"I'm not. I kissed him. Actually, he kissed me," I clarify. "It was so hot. And unexpected. But then he sort of ditched me."

"Well, now *this* is an interesting development." Tessa sits on the couch and tugs on Vi's arm until she plops down onto the cushion beside her. "Start from the beginning—you got to the studio, then what?"

With both sets of curious eyes boring into me, I recount my day at Bastien's studio, reliving the humiliation of trying on too-small clothes and the confusion when Sloane left me in the changing room.

"I couldn't tell if he was angry at himself for breaking one of his rules, or if he was embarrassed," I say, leaning on the arm of the couch that's opposite my friends.

Tessa shakes her head. "Henry Sloane doesn't seem like the type of man who gets embarrassed."

That's what I think too. "I just didn't expect him to kiss me like that and—"

The loud buzz of the apartment intercom halts our conversation.

Vi waggles her eyebrows. "Maybe that's Sloane looking to pick up where he left off."

"Oh, hell no. Can you imagine him in here? It's a dump compared to what he's used to." I glance at Tessa. "No offense." Crappy or not, thanks to her Nana—may she rest in peace—we've got a rent-controlled apartment that doesn't have a ton of hookers and hobos loitering out front. At last count, we were down to two regulars—Crystal and Candy—and Gus, a sweet homeless man who lives in the alley.

The buzzer sounds again, two short bursts this time. Holy impatient.

I press the button on the wall-mounted speaker. "Yes?"

"Hannah O'Keefe?"

"Yes, that's me."

Silence crackles through the speaker. "Don't test my patience. Check your fucking phone. You've got thirty minutes."

The intercom clicks off, and I turn to face a wide-eyed Vi and Tessa. Their palpable unease sends a surge of goosebumps up my arms. I grab my purse from where I dropped it beside the door and rifle through it until I find my phone. Fourteen missed texts and six calls. Shit.

"It's Davis. He wants the first payment by seven, or he's sending the video to Sloane."

"Oh my God." Vi steps forward and slides the chain lock into place on our door. "Is he coming up?"

Standing on her toes beside Violet, Tessa peers into the peephole.

"I didn't buzz him in," I say. Hopefully, no one else did either.

"Should we call the police?" Tessa asks, her eye still pressed against the door.

"Not yet. I think he's just trying to scare us." It's working. There's no way I'll leave this building without watching over my shoulder from now on.

I text a reply to Davis's last message.

I'll get you your money. No need to creep our apartment unless you want the police involved.

Davis's reply pops up within seconds.

Sloane would pay without being a bitch. I'll send it to him instead.

A vision of Sloane watching the video plays in my mind, and I panic. I can't let that happen. Not now. Not ever.

Wait. No Police. No Sloane. I'll send you the money in a second. $2K as agreed.

"Do you have enough?" Vi questions, reading over my shoulder.

"Barely. Mom sent me money for a plane ticket home. It was enough to cover the last bit I needed for this payment." A defeated sigh escapes my lips. "I'll go home once Davis has all his money. Only eight grand to go."

Tessa rests her hand on my shoulder. "What are you gonna do?"

"Get another job, I guess. I can't think of any easy get-rich-quick schemes, can you?"

"I could talk to Candy for you," Vi suggests. "As long as you don't mind working late and getting up early to go to your other job."

"Vi! Oh my God. I am *not* turning tricks with Candy! Are you kidding me, right now?"

"Not *that* Candy. Candace. The one who caters. She's always looking for people last minute when her staff call in sick. It's good money, I swear. I'd do it more often, but it usually interferes with my shift at the bar."

"I don't know." I hold up my hand like a waitress carrying a platter. "Can you imagine me trying to balance a tray of champagne? I'm such a klutz."

Tessa rechecks the deadbolt before backing away from the door. "Maybe you could do other things. Wash dishes or something. It's worth a shot, right?"

"I guess." My head lolls back as reality sets in. "Ah, hell, who am I kidding? I'd do almost anything right now."

My phone vibrates in my hand, and my gaze locks onto the screen. Above a video attachment, a message from Davis reads *Tick tock.* I click on the tiny triangle and point the phone toward my friends. "I can't let Sloane see this. Ever." Tapping my phone again, I stop the video. I can't stand to watch another second. I've had lots of opportunities to come clean to Sloane, but now I'm past the point of no return. Dealing with Davis is the consequence of that decision. I have to own it.

Scrolling through Davis's onslaught of messages, I follow his instructions to the letter and transfer two thousand dollars, cringing at the tiny balance left in my bank account.

***

Fourteen dollars doesn't get you far in New York City. For the next few days, I walk to Bastien's studio and stick to water for lunch. From this point forward, every penny counts, and food costs money I can't afford to spend.

By the time Friday morning rolls around, I'm more famished than tired, even after working a five-hour shift for

Candace. Turns out there's much more to catering than just passing around champagne. Hors d'oeuvres need serving, too. The only downside to that task is the smell. Those tiny fresh-baked treats wreak havoc on my diet willpower. To call it torture is an understatement. The only thing stopping me from binging is the two-pound loss on the scale. Even though I can't see a difference in the mirror, I'm happy enough with my progress that I splurge on a banana for breakfast.

When my first paycheck from Evans, Roth and Sloane doesn't hit my bank account by four, I'm desperate enough to sacrifice a subway token and make the trek to Human Resources to see what's going on. The possibility of running into Sloane helps to soften the inconvenience of the rush-hour voyage, especially since he hasn't been to Bastien's studio since our kiss.

"Your pay should clear before midnight," Sandra, the manager of HR assures me as I loiter near her desk. "Is everything okay?"

Her pitied expression makes me want to groan. It's the same look Mom gave me the first time she saw our apartment. She thinks we're living in the slums.

"I'm not concerned about the money," I lie. "I just happened to be in the area and wanted to check-in."

She nods. "Well, everything looks good to me. You go enjoy your weekend, dear."

"Thank you, Sandra. I will. I'm flying to California for the weekend. For fun," I add, for no other reason than to throw her off the idea that I'm poor. I don't know why it bothers me so much. I'm not *actually* poor; I'm financially challenged. It's temporary. Not everyone eats off a silver spoon when they're born, and I'm not afraid to work my way up to the top with good, old-fashioned hard work and determination.

Her eyes light up. "California? Which part? Most of my family lives there."

Crap. Damn my pride. I suck at geography. "San Francisco?" I inwardly cringe when it comes out more like a question. This is why lies are bad. One inevitably leads to the next until you're tangled in a web of mistruths.

"Yes! My sister is in Nob Hill. Ah, it's lovely there. Stop by when you're back, Hannah, I'd love to hear more about your trip."

"Okay, I will." Not. Turning on my heel, I point toward the elevator. "I'd better go. I haven't even packed yet." At least that's not utter bullshit.

"Have fun soaking up the California sun," she calls as I break into a brisk walk to avoid more questions.

"California sun?"

I skid to a halt at the sound of Sloane's voice and clutch my hand to my chest. "Jesus. You scared me."

"No, not Jesus. Just me."

A quiet laugh bubbles out of me before I can stop it. "You keep popping up out of nowhere. At some point, that's going to get a little creepy."

He grins. "Note taken. So, what's this about California?"

Meeting his stare, I consider lying but can't bring myself to do it. "It's a long story," I say, hoping he'll let the topic die.

"I have time."

Fuck. "Nah. It's very long and very boring, and I need to head home." At least that last part is mostly true. Candace called and asked me to work tonight, but my shift doesn't start until seven.

"Fair enough. I'll walk with you. I need to speak with you about something."

"Of course." Is this about our kiss? How could it not be?

In front of the bank of elevators, Sloane presses the button and stares up at the numbers on the digital display closest to us. They count down like a ticking time bomb. Fifty-eight. Fifty-seven.

My palms grow clammy as I wait for the inevitable. The talk. The one where he says our kiss was a mistake and can't happen again.

Fifty-six.

Say something, dammit. Rip it off quick. I can take it.

Fifty-five.

"Are you busy tomorrow night?" he asks, still watching the numbers tick by.

Fifty-four.

A date?

Fifty-three.

No. It can't be.

Fifty-two.

But what if it is?

The elevator arrives, and the doors slide open. I stare unblinking at the wall of suits inside, my mind stuck on Sloane's question.

"We'll catch the next one." Henry waves the people on before turning back to me. "Well?"

"Um, no. No, I'm not busy," I stammer.

"Good." Sloane taps on the down button again to call another elevator. "There's an event tomorrow night—an annual gala that Hudson Roth puts on for his investors. It's always a big to-do. You should go. Research for the 212 after-launch party. I haven't had a chance to talk to you about that yet, but I'd like your help to organize it."

"So, not a date?" My eyes jut open. "I mean, of course it's not a date." Ah, Jesus.

"Still not Jesus."

I look away and close my eyes. Fucking Christ almighty. What the hell is wrong with me? Another elevator dings at our back, and I squeeze my way into the already overcrowded space. "I'll go," I tell him, ignoring his shit-eating grin.

"Good. I'll send you the details." He sticks his hand in his pocket, all casual like he does in his famous suit ads. "Don't be late."

CHAPTER *nine*

Fuck my life.

Fuck my luck.

Fuck my idiotic friends who got me into this godforsaken mess.

"Please, Hannah," Violet begs. "Candace is desperate. Two thousand dollars each. And you can have half of my share."

"Half of mine, too," Tessa adds, hanging the skimpy dress she's holding back onto the sale rack. We've spent the better part of the day cruising stores for a dress for me to wear to the gala when Candace's panicked call changes all our plans. A bunch of her staff have caught the flu, and now she needs servers for a business function tonight.

Vi wiggles four fingers in front of my face. "Count 'em, Hannah. That's four thousand dollars. Imagine the dent that will make in what you owe Davis."

I sigh. She's right. Of course, she's right, but dammit, I was looking forward to being a guest tonight and not the hired staff.

"What about Sloane?" I whine, one last-ditch effort to make them see where I'm coming from. My head says take the money, but my heart aches at the chance to see Sloane. "It's going to look so bad that I'm bailing on him last minute."

Tessa waves away my concern with the swipe of her hand. "Tell him you're sick. Has he even sent you the details yet?"

"No. But—"

"Then it can't be that important. You don't even know if he's going to the gala. He said it was for research."

"I know, but—"

The musical ringtone of Violet's cell halts our conversation. She glances at the screen before looking back at me. "It's Candace. You in or not?" Her eyebrows disappear under the fringe of her bangs as she stares at me.

"Fine," I groan. "Yes, I'm in. I'll email Sloane and let him know that I won't be there."

"She's in," Vi says into her phone. "No problem, Candace. And thanks." Vi slips the device back into her purse. "She's sending a cab to pick us up at four."

"What? That's in two hours!" I squeak. "Three of us and just one bathroom. We need to go—now!"

Vi nudges Tessa before leaning in close to her ear. "I'll shower with you—to save time and water."

The sly grin Tessa returns makes me smile. God, those two are horndogs.

"I'm going first," I say. "I don't trust you guys to not get carried away."

The melodic lilt of Tessa's laugh floats between us. She

peeks over at Vi. "No funny business, okay?"

"*Me?*" She feigns innocence. "It's always you who starts it."

***

By some miracle, all three of us are showered and ready before the cab arrives. I check my phone again while we wait, but Sloane still hasn't responded to my email. Not even a *feel better soon*, considering I gave him a sob story about eating bad Chinese food.

At the Plaza Hotel, we enter through a small side entrance and find Candace waiting for us just inside the door. "You're here! Thank you. Oh my god, do I owe you big time." She points toward several dresses hanging on the coat rack, all of them still covered in a film of plastic. "Uniforms are over there. Once you've changed, come find me, and I'll get you guys set up for the night. We're still short a few bodies, but we'll have to make do. Like I told Vi, this gig is *huge* for me. If it goes smoothly, I'm splitting the bonus between the twelve of us. If it tanks, I'm bankrupt. Literally. All my eggs are in this basket, so I apologize now if I yell at you later. It's just the stress. Please don't take it personally." Candace glances at her watch. "Okay. Enough blabbing. Go change. Let's get this party started!"

***

Within thirty minutes of the first few guests filing in, we seem to have found our groove. Vi delivers trays of champagne to the guests like a seasoned pro and Tessa follows in her path, collecting empties. Like the last few events I worked for Candace, I make my way through the crowd serving bite-sized pastries while trying to convince my stomach the food isn't meant for me.

"Well, hello, beautiful. I'll take one of those," a male voice purrs with a slight nasal whine.

I slow to a stop and keep my eye roll to myself. These types of comments are nothing new, but in my limited experience, they usually come closer to the end of the night. Turning to face the short, paunchy man, I take in his burgundy pinstripe suit and try to keep from laughing. I smile politely and lower the tray to his level, but what I really want to do is let him know that Austin Powers called and he wants his suit back.

"You are stunning," he tells me—or rather, he says to my breasts.

I hold out a napkin and ignore his comment. "Serviette?"

"Thank you, sweetie." His fingers graze my hand in a not-so-subtle move as he takes it.

Withdrawing my hand, I force a smile and take a step away. "You're welcome, sir. Enjoy the rest of your evening."

Back in the kitchen, I grab a new tray, this one a mix of crackers topped with a smooth pink spread. My stomach gurgles. "God, I'm starving," I mumble to myself. The broccoli I had for lunch has long since digested.

Vi steps up beside me and steals a cracker from the tray. "Mmm, oh, man that's good," she moans, tiny flecks of cracker spilling from her mouth as she speaks.

"Hey," I admonish. "Stop that."

"No one's gonna know." She leans in close. "It's payment for having my ass touched all night by men who can't tell I'm batting for the other team." She wrinkles her nose. "All they see are tits and ass."

"I know, right? Two guys already asked me what time I get off."

"Ugh," she groans. "I swear, the richer they are, the more entitled they think they are to touch. I'd slap some of these men if it wouldn't get me fired."

"No one gets slapped, ladies. Let's keep it professional." Candace appears behind us.

Vi scrunches up her face, grimacing guiltily as she takes another tray of champagne flutes and disappears into the ballroom.

A ripple of dizziness washes over me, and I lean against the edge of the counter for support. I breathe in deep through my nose and exhale slowly. I meant to eat something small before we left but ran out of time.

"Everything good, Hannah?" Candace asks.

I nod. "Yeah. Just a little lightheaded. I'm fine. I should get back out there, too."

She hums under her breath. "You've got me worried now. You'd better not come down with what the others have got. At least not until after tonight. No offense."

"I'm good. It's just this crazy low-cal, low-carb, low-fat diet I'm on."

"What? Why? And what the hell does that leave you to eat?"

"Not much. But it works."

"Oh, Hannah. Here." She hands me a cracker. "Eat this. No fainting allowed, got it?"

I take the cracker and give her a tight-lipped smile. "I'm good. Honest."

As quickly as she appeared, Candace disappears to take care of something else. I toss the high-carb treat in the garbage and grab the tray of hors d'oeuvres. Lightheaded or not, I'm not about to cheat on my diet.

Back in the ballroom, I make several passes through the crowd and switch out my empty platter for a new one, this one covered in bite-sized chocolate desserts drizzled in raspberry.

Moments into my third trip, I stop mid-step and suck in a breath. What are the chances?

Across the room, Sloane stands on the outskirts, deep in conversation with a willowy brunette. Her bright-red dress clings to her lithe, little body, so tight, I swear I can see her ribs. She throws her head back and laughs, her hand grasping at Sloane's forearm as if what he's said is so hilarious she needs his help to keep her upright. My heart thrashes against my rib cage in a jealous fit. Is this what he wants in a woman—a real-life Scarlett O'Hara? No matter how many calories I cut, I'll never be that petite. I have hips. An hourglass figure that I'm told men love—just not the man I want.

I make a move to turn away before he sees me, but I'm too late. Sloane glances up from his discussion and locks onto my gaze. His brow furrows.

Dammit, I'm done. I can't lie my way out of this one, not after the detailed email I sent him about how sick I was feeling.

In a moment of panic, I turn to escape, but a woman around my age stops me. She reaches for a chocolate square, pausing momentarily to ask if they contain nuts.

"They don't," I tell her. "They're also gluten-free."

She hums. "Well, maybe just a small one."

While she takes her time to choose from the equally-sized squares, I peek over her shoulder at Sloane. His one-on-one with Scarlett O'Hara has turned into a threesome, the newest member of his fan club a tall redhead with a model's figure.

Poor Sloane. What a predicament. How will he choose

which one to take home?

Ugh. Who am I kidding? He could take both. I bet they'd do anything to share a bed with Henry Sloane. Fuck. I'd do anything to share a bed with Henry—.

"Mmmm, a woman after my heart," a nasal voice says behind me.

I turn to face the same portly man from earlier.

He winks at me. "When given a choice, I'll always choose dessert." He takes one of the chocolate squares from the tray and pops it in his mouth, then licks his stubby fingers and takes another.

Gross.

"You have very pretty hair. It suits you."

"Thank you." Taking a small step in the opposite direction, I try to outmaneuver his outstretched hand, but the guests to my back make that impossible.

He tucks a few strands of loose hair behind my ear. "There. Much better." He grins at me, remnants of the brown dessert coating his front tooth like an ill-colored crown. "I don't normally do this, but I'm hosting a private party at my home next Saturday. I was wondering if—"

I shake my head before he has the chance to ask me anything. "I'm sorry. I can't. I've already committed to working another event that day," I lie.

"And, if she's not working, she'll either be in California or have food poisoning, isn't that right, Hannah?"

Shit. I force my face into an expression I hope doesn't resemble my surprise at Sloane's terse voice in my ear. One thing is for certain—he's not happy with me.

"Please, excuse us." Sloane takes my arm, directing me

away from my paunchy friend, and leads us down a narrow corridor.

I smile sheepishly and hold up the platter of desserts. "Want one? They're gluten-free."

"Stop the bullshit, Hannah," he grits.

The terseness in his voice makes me flinch.

"I asked HR for your cell number to text you the address for tonight. Imagine my surprise when Sandra said not to bother, that you were flying to California for the weekend—*for fun.*"

My teeth play at my bottom lip. I knew that lie would come back to bite me. It was completely unnecessary.

"And then this afternoon, I got your very long-winded, very detailed account of your unfortunate case of food poisoning— also a lie, I presume?"

My shoulders fall. "I'm sorry. I can explain."

He shakes his head. "Don't bother. Why are you even here —*working?*"

"It's just that I…" My words trail off as a sudden wave of dizziness hits me without warning. I slump against the wall, grateful for the support, and try to keep my tray from toppling.

"Hannah?"

Through the steady whooshing in my ears, I make out what sounds like my name as the tray disappears from my grip.

Leaning forward, I brace my elbows on my thighs. This usually helps. "I just need a minute," I whisper.

After the wave of dizziness subsides, I slowly stand upright but continue staring at the floor. My fingers play at the short hem of my uniform, and I subtly wipe the layer of sweat from my palms on the fabric. Except for the damage to my pride, I think I've mostly recovered.

"Look at me," Sloane says, his tone more concerned than angry.

Forcing my eyes upward, I meet his steely gaze, his usual aqua blues appearing slate gray in the muted light of the hallway. Even in my groggy state, I can't stop myself from admiring his handsome features, the perfectly groomed scruff on his jaw. It's no wonder he was a model. He's beautiful.

With his finger under my chin, he tips my head up farther and studies my face. He thinks I'm faking. And why wouldn't he? I've already proven myself to be a liar.

At the end of the hallway, Tessa rounds the corner and skids to a halt. "There you are. You nearly passed out again, didn't you?" When she reaches us, she glances at Sloane. "It's this stupid diet she's on."

His brows draw together. "Stay with her. I'll be right back."

When Tessa nods, Sloane takes off down the hallway at a steady clip, taking my tray with him, and heading in the direction of the kitchen.

"Oh, no, what is he doing?" I mumble, forcing myself to speak. "He's going to get me fired." A new wave of dizziness rolls through me, along with a surge of nausea that claws at my gut. I curl over, clutching my stomach, and groan.

Tessa rubs circles on my back. "He won't. Candace is worried about you. She said you had a little spell in the kitchen."

"I did, but I'm fine, Tessa, really." I take a moment to collect my breath as the nauseousness subsides then stand upright. "I'm good now."

"You need to eat, Hannah. Come on. You're going to kill yourself trying to lose weight you don't need to lose!"

"I'm not. I just—ugh—I want to feel good in my body. You should see the women I work with. God. They're tiny, perfect little humans who could probably get modeling contracts if they wanted to."

"I don't believe it," Tessa says, shaking her head. "Nobody's perfect. And you shouldn't want to be either. You're the one who's always telling me it's my quirks that make me *me*."

"Sloane is perfect," I whisper, more to myself than her.

As if conjured from my words, Henry appears at my side again, back from wherever he went. "How is she?" he asks Tessa.

"She's not good. She needs to go home and eat."

I meet her eyes. "Traitor."

Tessa smiles. "Sorry, babe. Gotta call it like it is."

With his hand on my lower back, Sloane leads me down the hallway, turning at the end toward the exit instead of the ballroom. "Come on."

"No. Where are we going? I can't leave." I need the money.

"You can—and you are. I've already talked to Candace." He hooks his arm around my waist and pulls me into his side. "I'm taking you home."

CHAPTER
ten

In the passenger seat of Sloane's Maserati, I lay my head against the soft, cool leather and close my eyes. My stomach churns. I fight against the queasiness, breathing through each wave until it's gone.

I'm dreaming of biting into a big, juicy burger when the sudden aroma of fast food floods my senses. I open my eyes, disoriented and confused but also famished.

Outside my window, we roll past rows of concrete pillars and luxury cars. We're underground. "Where are we?" I croak.

"Hey, you're awake," Sloane says, pulling into an empty parking space. "How are you feeling?"

I swipe at the hair stuck to my sweat-covered forehead and peek over at him. "Not the greatest." I haven't felt this shaky since the last time I had the flu. I'm a mess. And I hate that he's seeing me like this. "Where did you say we are again?"

"I didn't." He glances out his window. "You fell asleep. And I didn't have your address, so I brought you back to my place."

"Oh." That makes sense. I lay my head back on the seat, secretly relieved. It's bad enough that he's seeing *me* at my worst, he doesn't need to see my apartment too. Crystal and Candy would have a two-for-one special in place before he even came to a complete stop in front of the building.

I gesture to the paper bag on the console between us. "That smells delicious, by the way. What'd you get?"

"Burgers and fresh-cut fries. Best in New York City. I bought two of everything, so I hope you plan to eat."

My stomach roils. As hungry as I am, the thought of heavy food in my belly makes me uneasy. "Not sure about that, but I'll try."

Sloane rounds the car before I have a chance to undo my seatbelt and opens my door. Slow and steady, I'm careful not to stand up too fast. I really do need to eat. I feel awful.

I follow Sloane to the elevator, and we ride up to the penthouse suite. The doors open to a spacious vestibule that takes my breath away. It looks straight out to the City skyline. I slip off my heels and head straight to the bank of floor-to-ceiling windows.

"It's incredible. That's Central Park," I muse, pointing to the forest of trees in the distance.

"It is."

"You live in a fairytale," I tell him. Moving around the generous living room, I admire every detail. The art on his walls is an interesting mix of contemporary and classic, but somehow it works. It suits the space—it suits *him*. Intricate white molding lines every window, doorway and wall, and fresh-cut flower arrangements carry my eye to key focal points around the room. The entire place is beautiful and classy, and not at all what I imagined a bachelor pad to look like.

"Here, eat." Sloane hands me a plate with the biggest burger I've ever seen.

He plops down on a nearby off-white couch, and I sit on the matching one opposite him. "We shouldn't be eating in here. It's too nice."

He shrugs. "It's leather. It wipes off."

I shake my head. And there's the bachelor side of him I was wondering about. I bite into a fry and hum. They are good. Some of the tastiest fries I've ever had, in fact.

"Don't forget the ranch dressing." He hands me a small, round tub of sauce. "You haven't lived until you've dipped fries in this."

"Ugh," I groan. "You're killing me. I can't eat all this. But thank you."

"Try it. You won't be disappointed." Setting his plate down on his lap, he waits and watches as I open the tiny container and dip in one of my fries.

He's right. I pop the rest of the French fry into my mouth. Mmmm. The moan I make sounds unholy. "So good, Sloane, oh my god." My eyes pop open. "Mr. Sloane? I'm sorry."

He smiles. "Don't. I like that you call me Sloane."

"All right. Good." Picking up the burger, I hold it up to survey the enormous hunk of meat. "I'm not even sure how to wrap my mouth around this thing."

His eyes twinkle with amusement. "That's what she said."

A violent laugh escapes me before I can stop it. I can't believe he said that.

Once I've hauled my head out of the gutter, I glance at Sloane to see how he's tackling the sizable burger. He dives right in, taking another healthy bite.

"Here goes." I open as wide as I can and manage to get some of the burger and bun inside my mouth. "So good," I mumble, my mouth still full. "Mmmmm."

Sloane watches from his seat across from me, seemingly amused by my theatrics. He polishes off his burger before I can make a dent in mine.

Before I get too full, I stand from the couch and wander toward the beautiful kitchen that overlooks the living room. "Thank you for the food," I say, envying the exorbitant amount of cupboard space he has compared to our tiny apartment. "I really needed to eat." Drawing a deep breath, I set my plate of leftovers on the counter and adjust the waistband of my pantyhose. "Ugh, I think I ate too much," I groan.

Sloane chuckles. "You barely ate!"

On my way back to the couch, my stomach makes an ominous noise, and I stop mid-step. Saliva floods the back of my throat, and I have to keep swallowing to make it go away. "Oh god," I whisper.

"You all right over there?"

Sweat pools on my forehead as another wave of nausea rolls through me. "Um, can I use your bathroom?"

"Of course." He points down the hallway. "Second door on your left."

Inside the swanky space, I stand at the sink and throw water on my face. It's going to mess up my makeup, but I'm more concerned about not losing my dinner in Sloane's fancy toilet.

"Ugh," I groan. The initial pleasure of the tasty burger has long worn off, and now it sits heavy in my belly. I stare at my reflection. I look like shit and feel ten times worse. I have a funny feeling this night won't bode well for me.

Out of nowhere, my stomach lurches to my throat, and I run to the toilet, barely making it in time to open the lid and toss the contents of my gut.

Over and over, I bow to the porcelain gods, pausing every so often to blow my nose and wipe the sweat from my forehead.

Sloane knocks on the door, asking if I'm all right and I tell him yes, I just need a second.

By the time my body has finished retching, I can barely hold my head up. Sinking to the ground, I press my cheek to the cool tile floor and sigh. It feels so good. All I need is a few minutes down here, and I'll be fine.

***

The digital clock beside my head flashes an ungodly hour. Four o'clock. Jesus. I make a move to roll over to my other side but don't make it past my back. A wicked pounding assaults my temples. "Ouch."

"Hey. You're awake."

Careful not to make any sudden moves, I slowly turn my head on the feather-soft pillow and find Sloane lying next to me.

"How are you feeling, Hannah?"

I groan. "Like I've been hit by a truck."

"Let me get you some meds." He climbs off the mattress and disappears through the doorway on my side of the bed, returning with two small pills in his palm. "Can you sit up?"

With the speed of a tortoise, I push myself up and lay my head back against the headboard. Dressed down in pajama pants and a white t-shirt, Sloane looks as good in pajamas as he does in a suit. No fair.

He hands me a glass of water from the table beside me, and I swallow the medicine before tugging at my tight black dress. Damn uniform.

"Here." Sloane sets a folded t-shirt on the bedspread. "I'll give you some privacy to change. No point in taking you home this late." He pauses in the doorway. "Oh, I answered your phone earlier, I hope that's okay. It was your friend, Tessa. I told her where you are and that you're safe. I'll drop you home tomorrow once you're feeling up to it."

I sigh again. "Thank you for doing that. I'm sorry for ruining your night."

He waves away my apology. "Don't be. I'm not much of a caretaker, I'm afraid."

"You're doing good." Better than good. His level of care makes me like him even more. Cut-throat businessman or not, he's a real sweetheart.

"I'll be back in a few minutes to check on you." He winks. "Don't worry, I'll knock."

Sloane leaves, and I struggle with my dress before tossing the t-shirt to the foot of the bed. It's no use. With the zipper at my back, I only manage to get it down an inch before curling into a fetal position. Another wave of nausea hits me, less ferocious than before, but still uncomfortable. There's nothing left to throw up, but sometimes that's so much worse.

As promised, Sloane knocks on the door when he returns.

"Come in."

His brow furrows when he sees me. "Aww, you're stuck," he says, seemingly amused by my predicament. "Let me help you." Henry moves to the side of the bed and gently pulls me up until I'm sitting. "Still good?

I nod.

"All right. Let's see." Moving my hair away from the zipper, he meets my gaze as he slowly slides it down.

I imagine him unzipping my dress for any other reason and hold back a moan. My fantasy has morphed into a nightmare.

Sloane hands me back the t-shirt that I threw away. "Give it another try. I'll be right back."

Once the bedroom door closes, I strip off the dress, along with my pantyhose and bra and find instant relief. So much better. Bringing his t-shirt to my nose, I inhale Sloane's scent before pulling the soft fabric over my head. Mmmm. Even his clean laundry smells like him.

Exhausted from the workout of changing, I lie down on top of the covers and rest my eyes.

***

The next time I wake, the room is bright with sunshine. I wipe my hand across my mouth and groan. The sour taste of bile on my tongue disgusts me.

Beside me, the covers shuffle.

I turn my head, a nice, slow movement to keep the throbbing at bay. Sloane watches me from his pillow, his eyes still sleep-ridden.

"What time is it?" I say, pausing to clear my scratchy throat.

"Noon." He yawns. "Ah, I'm sorry. I didn't sleep well."

"I'm the one who's sorry. God, this is so embarrassing," I croak, my voice seriously frog-like. "I puked in your bathroom. That's just so, so wrong."

He smiles. "That's nothing compared to your breath."

My eyes grow wide. I slap my palm over my mouth and roll

to my side. "Oh my god."

The heat of his hand on my back does nothing to console me. "I'm joking, Hannah. I can't smell your breath from here." He rubs small circles. "Though it's probably putrid." He chuckles. "There's a new toothbrush on the bathroom counter for you. Toothpaste is in the drawer."

Ignoring my pounding head, I roll out of bed and hightail it to the bathroom as his laughter continues. Jerk.

After a thorough brush of my teeth, I stare at my reflection. The girl in the mirror doesn't even look like me. It looks like death stole her away then spit her out 'cause she wasn't quite ready.

I wash my face over the sink, but it's not enough. Taking liberties I don't deserve, I step into the heaven that is his shower. Water hits me from every direction, and I stand under the spray for what feels like forever. I'm not sure if it's the steam or the heavy pounding of the water on my back, but I feel more like myself when I get out.

Except I'm still at Sloane's. And I spent the night puking in his bathroom.

I sigh. If at some point he liked me, even a little, that's probably gone. You don't watch someone puke their guts out and suddenly grow more fond of them. Life doesn't work that way, especially for sexy men who could have any pick of the crop. I bet he wishes he went home with Scarlett O'Hara.

And, to make matters worse, now that I've showered, I'm entirely makeup-free. He's about to see me *au naturel.* The only makeup I've got is clear lip gloss in my purse.

After drying myself off with a towel, I slip back into his t-shirt and my panties and peek outside the bathroom door.

Sloane is nowhere to be seen. Thank God.

I pad slowly down his hallway, hesitant for Sloane to see me, but eager to have a taste of whatever he's cooking. It smells divine.

When I enter the kitchen, he turns to face me, a spatula in his hand. As if he couldn't get any sexier—he can cook. He looks like a natural in the kitchen, a worn pair of jeans sitting low on his hips, a light-gray t-shirt hugging his chest.

I silently swoon.

"Hi." My fingers play at the hem of his t-shirt that barely covers my ass. "I used your shower."

"I see that. Feeling better?"

"So much better. Thank you." That nice, hot shower made all the difference. "What are you making? It smells amazing."

He turns back to the stove and scrapes the contents of the pan onto two plates already covered in salad. "Marinated chicken and mixed greens. I thought you might want something light."

Combing my fingers through my hair, I push the damp strands back over my shoulders and take a seat on one of his barstools. "Sounds perfect. I'm starving." But this time I'm only going to have a little bit in case it comes right back up. "You're a better caretaker than you give yourself credit for."

Sloane sets a plate of food in front of me and takes the empty seat beside me. "I have my mom to thank for that. She raised us to be independent boys." He laughs. "And now she complains that we're *too* independent."

I grin. "Aww. Are you close with your family?"

"Yeah. We all live within a block of Central Park. My bother and I joke that Mom won't let us move away. What about you?

Siblings?"

My head shakes. "Nah, just me. I'm close with my parents, too, but it's been a while since I've seen them." I grimace. "It's been nearly a year since I went home." Guilt niggles at my gut. I really need to make a better effort to see them more.

"Well, don't wait too long to visit," he says, his gaze dipping to my lap. "Life is short…" Sloane shakes his head. "…Way too short." He clears his throat and takes a sip of water, looking away. "So, 212. I'd love to hear your ideas. We need a catchy tagline."

"I've been thinking about that, too. I figure we'll know it when we hear it. When you know, you know. *You know?*" I grin.

He nods but doesn't smile at my dorky joke.

We fall into a stretch of awkward silence, and I spend the rest of the meal contemplating what I've done wrong.

Glancing over, I catch him staring at my legs again. The way I'm sitting, his t-shirt barely touches my thighs. I tug it down as best as I can. "I couldn't find my clothes," I explain.

His gaze drifts up to mine, his expression serious. "I can't do this." He balls his fists. "I can't let you sit here in my kitchen all damp hair and practically naked."

Okay, so *that's* what's wrong. "You want me to go." I slide off the barstool just as he stands from his, and we end up cocooned between both chairs.

"No." His fingertips brush across my cheek. "I want you to *not* go. And therein lies my dilemma."

Peering up at his bright blue eyes, a quiet *oh* finds its way past my lips.

"If I kiss you, I don't trust myself to stop."

"Then don't," I breathe.

With a minute shake of his head, his resolve begins to crumble. "Don't encourage me, Hannah."

"I can't help it." I run the pad of my thumb across his bottom lip and lower my voice to a whisper. "I want you, Sloane."

His Adam's apple bobs in his throat as he swallows.

He's hesitant.

He's got rules.

"Please, Henry."

My whispered plea is met by the crashing of his lips against mine. I grab his shirt in my fist, and he moans into my mouth, his fingers threading tightly through my hair.

I match his enthusiasm, our tongues lashing at each other, exploring. I knew it would be like this. Fiery. Passionate. Raw.

Henry lifts me into his arms as if I'm featherlight, and I instinctively wrap my legs around him while he carries me down the hallway. The gritty moan that leaves his throat makes me clench. If I'm dreaming, God, please don't wake me up.

He deposits me on his mattress, and my damp hair fans out across his bedspread. I peer up at him, watching and waiting for his next move. I don't want to miss a thing.

Reaching behind his shoulders, he pulls off his shirt and shucks his pants in record time. He climbs onto the bed, and my eyes trace the ridges of his chiseled abs, following them down to the fine trail of hair that disappears into his boxer-briefs.

My body shivers in anticipation. I need this. I need *him*.

Scooting up the bed, I lay my head on his pillow and Sloane kneels between my legs. He kisses my lips then pushes my shirt up slowly past my breasts. "Mmmm," he hums. "Pale pink." His mouth descends on my breast, and I writhe under the weight of his body until he pinches my other nipple. "Keep still, baby."

His fingers slip inside my panties, and I cry out as he goes straight for my clit, his thumb circling mercilessly around the tiny bud. "You're all wet for me."

I clutch at the bedsheets. "Yes," I whisper with a breathless sigh. "Oh my god."

Moving up on the bed, he kisses my neck, sucking on the sensitive spot beneath my ear. He pushes two fingers inside me, and I buck up off the mattress, moaning so loud I'd be embarrassed if I weren't so close to coming.

"That's it," he says. "Give it to me, Hannah. Make a mess all over my fingers."

His filthy words push me past the final hurdle, and I detonate, thrashing against his hand as I come.

Reaching between us, I rub his cock through the fabric of his underwear. He's big. Thick and long, and part of me worries that it might hurt me.

"Over the edge of the mattress—" he kisses my lips "—or you on top?"

Biting my lip, I stare into his eyes as I decide. "I've never tried it from behind before."

"Never?" He moans as I move into position, bent over the side of the bed, my ass on display for him. I'm open and exposed, and it adds an extra layer of excitement.

The warmth of his hands on my back sends goosebumps skittering over my skin. Every part of me is on high alert, in tune with every place his body touches mine. His palms move down to my ass, his big strong hands smoothing over each of my cheeks. Leaning over me, he sweeps my hair away from my ear. "Have you ever been spanked, Hannah?"

I shake my head, my face heating to epic proportion.

"Mmmm," he hums, lowering his voice. "Maybe next time."

Next time? Oh, hell, yes.

Behind me, the crinkling of a wrapper gives me pause. Condom? Yes, thank God someone's on the ball. In my lust-filled haze, I'd completely forgotten.

"Ready?" His fingers play at my folds, and I clench.

"Uh-huh," I manage. Long past ready.

In one agonizingly slow motion, Sloane pushes inside me, stopping once he's fully seated. I take a breath as I adjust to his size.

Sloane slides himself out to the tip and stops again.

"No," I mewl. "Don't stop."

"Tell me how bad you need it, Hannah," he says, his gravel-filled voice low and rumbly.

"I'm desperate for you. Please." I wriggle beneath him, trying to satisfy my ache. "Please fuck me."

His fingers tighten on my hips and mine clutch at the sheets, waiting. And then he strikes. Slamming inside me, thrusting in long, hard strokes that press my thighs into the mattress.

I cry out, loud and wild, my hips bucking back to meet him. "Oh, yes. God. Please," I beg. "I'm close." Embarrassingly close. I never come this fast. And never twice.

"Wait," Sloane chokes. "Not yet."

Gripping my hips, he pulls me back to him, over and over until I can't hold back any longer. "I'm—ohhh," I moan. "I'm coming."

With one last thrust, Sloane slams into me and groans, a loud guttural sound that makes me cry out again. Leaning forward, he stays inside me and latches onto my shoulder with his teeth.

He soothes the bite mark with a kiss. "You're so fucking beautiful, Hannah."

When he finally pulls out, we climb back onto the bed to catch our breaths. Staring up at the ceiling, I lie beside my sexy, sweaty, naked boss.

I fucked Henry Sloane—and it was goddamn glorious.

CHAPTER *eleven*

For the past two weeks, Sloane and I have taken to fucking every chance we get. In his office. In his bed. In his shower. That man is insatiable.

After an hour-long marathon that starts in the kitchen and ends with me pinned against his shower wall, I leave Sloane in his bed and head to his kitchen to find us a snack. Following what I now call *the puking incident at Sloane's*, I did some soul-searching and came to the conclusion that eating next to nothing is a terrible way to lose weight. It's not healthy in the long run, and it makes me miserable. I'm much happier now, eating smaller portions of whatever I want and counting sex as cardio.

I hunt through Henry's fridge, organizing some of the condiments in the door while I look for something for us to eat. Not wanting to ruin our dinner, I opt for yogurt and fresh-cut berries then return to his room with two coffee mugs filled with our snack.

"For you," I say, presenting him his mug and spoon with a t-shirt curtsy.

His eyebrow quirks. "Thanks. Interesting bowl you've got there."

I shrug. "We never have enough dishes at the apartment, and now it's normal. It's handy, though, right?" I hold the mug up by the handle. "Less chance of dropping it, too. I'm a little bit klutzy, in case you haven't noticed."

He grins.

"Of course, you've noticed." I match his smile. "I'm pretty impressed neither of us has endured a sex injury yet."

His eyebrow ticks upward a second time, and I laugh.

"Odds are, it will be *you* injured," I warn. "And *me* the culprit doing the injuring."

"Good to know."

"Oh, shoot, I forgot something." Setting my yogurt on his nightstand, I run back to his kitchen and return with our drinks. I prance around to his side of the bed and pass him a wine glass. "It's just water," I tell him.

His hand slips under the bottom of my shirt once I'm close enough, and he grabs my bum. "I love watching you parade around in just my t-shirt. Looks good on you. You've got great legs." He glances up at my head. "The hair could use some work."

"Hey!" I move across his room to look in the mirror. When we'd finished in the shower, I'd pulled my hair into a messy, wet bun, but now it's flopped to one side with wisps of hair falling around my neck. "Ah, whatever," I shrug. "This is me."

"For the record, I like you exactly the way you are."

I stoop to kiss his lips. "You're sweet." I poke at his reading glasses. "These are cute."

"*I* am not cute."

"You're cute, Sloane. Accept it. Now, say it with me: *This is me.*" I take the wine glass from his grip when he doesn't comply and set it on his nightstand. "Come on, say it. *This is me.*"

With an exasperated shake of his head, he entertains me and waves his hand over his body. "This is me."

I wrinkle my nose. "Nah. Didn't convince me."

"This is me," he says more serious. "Now get over here before I take you over the edge of the bed and spank you for being a brat."

Grinning, I grab my yogurt, and I climb back onto the bed, seating myself at the foot of the mattress so I can face him. "That's not exactly an incentive to behave, you know."

"I know. I'm just happy you're finally starting to see yourself through my eyes. You don't need to change a thing about you. And you definitely don't need to diet. You're perfect the way you are."

"Thanks. I figure I need to accept that I am who I am. Imperfections and all. *This is me.*"

In a moment of clarity, I see the entire 212 campaign unfolding before my eyes.

"*This is me,*" I say, in awe. "That's it."

"What's it?"

"The tag line. For 212." I climb off the bed, depositing my yogurt back onto the nightstand. "Imagine this." I hold my hands out in front of me as if that might help me explain what I see in my head. "Photos of all of the models—different shapes, heights, abilities, ethnicities, and ages—all wearing an outfit from the new extended women's line. We could record video clips of each of them saying *This is me*." I pace his bedroom, brainstorming my ideas aloud. "Positive body image is huge these days."

"I like that," Henry says. "It's perfect."

I plop down on the bed, relief flooding my system. "I wish I had my MacBook with me. I want to start mocking up the designs."

"It's brilliant. You're the whole package, Hannah. Brains, beauty. Quirks," he adds with a smile.

I laugh. "Well, *this is me*," I joke. "If you don't like it, you can suck it."

He lunges at me and pushes me down onto the mattress. "Don't mind if I do."

***

I'm so busy fucking Sloane and planning the marketing campaign for 212 that I almost forget to send Davis his next payment. His thirty-day deadline is looming, but I'm still nearly a thousand dollars short.

Just sent you another $1,800. That's all I've got at the moment.

Hoping that deposit will put Davis in a good mood, I quickly add on to my message.

I might need an extension.

I'm on the way to Bastien's studio for the big photoshoot when my phone buzzes with his reply.

No. Deadline stands. Friday. 7 p.m.

I sigh. I should have spent less time fucking Sloane and more time working for Candace. While the four thousand dollars helped a lot, my opportunities to work with Candace have dwindled.

Inside Bastien's studio, I make my way through the building. The place is buzzing with staff and models of every shape and size. My heart is bursting at the seams with giddiness at seeing my ideas come together so quickly. Sloane's been so supportive, and for the most part, he's let me run with it.

I wave at Trista as I approach. She stands at Bastien's side as he makes an adjustment to an emerald green dress on one of the plus-size models. Leila. I recognize her stunning green eyes from the applications. She looks amazing.

We've come so far in just thirty days. I never thought we'd reach the point where even Bastien would come around so completely. He's done a one-eighty and seems proud to be heading up the fashion designs. It helps that the news outlets have been all over this story, and all over the man behind the designs. The concept of such a high-end brand catering to more than the one percent is almost unheard of. In this day and age, it shouldn't be news, but it is. And I'll take it. So will Sloane. He's happy to let Bastien have his ego stroked by the journalists if it keeps him happy and willing to work on future projects with Evans, Roth and Sloane.

"You look beautiful," I tell Leila with a smile.

She blushes. "Thanks. This is so weird. Dresses always make me feel frumpy, but not this one."

"This isn't just a dress. It's art," Bastien says. "And *I* am the artiste. They don't call me a fashion aficionado for nothing."

Leila's confused expression makes me grin. "What Bastien's trying to say, is that you look gorgeous. That color really brings out the green in your eyes."

"Thanks." She clasps her hands together and wrings her

fingers. "I'm nervous. I'm not a model, and I've never walked on a runway before. What if I trip?"

"You won't. And the whole point of this campaign is to showcase everyday women. Everyone we hired for this shoot has never modeled. It was one of the criteria we used to make sure the campaign is authentic."

Her shoulders drop as she visibly relaxes. "Ok, good. Thank you for telling me that."

I smile. "The runway that's set up here is the same one that will be assembled on July first. We'll do as many takes as we need to to get the shots for our creatives. So, no pressure. And I'm sure Bastien won't mind if you come back over the next few weeks to practice walking the runway—right, Bastien?"

He stands from his kneeled stoop. "Yes. But check in with Trista first." With the flick of his wrist, Bastien directs Leila to join the rest of the models who've assembled for today's shoot. "You're ready. Let's get started."

Bastien leads the four of us to the other side of the studio where an area has been staged to record video footage and take still shots of each of the models.

A long catwalk has been built, just as we'd discussed, along with staged areas that resemble real-life work locations. An office boardroom. A classroom. A bank.

In front of the faux office setup, a cameraman records video as a scene plays out. The model—a woman with a prosthetic leg —stands at the front of the boardroom. But instead of standing behind the podium provided, she hosts her faux presentation beside it. Her turquoise silk blouse is paired with a black pencil skirt and three-inch heels that match her shirt. She looks at the camera, breaking the fourth wall, and says, "This is me."

The director cuts the scene, and everyone breaks into applause. Goosebumps swarm my skin. Everything about this campaign gives me the feels.

A hand slips into mine, and I peek over at Sloane. "Hi," I whisper. He smiles, running his thumb over my skin as we watch the photographer take photos of the same model.

By the time four o'clock rolls around, we've captured photos and video of fourteen different models, all ranging in size from double zero to sixteen. My heart swells with pride. Four weeks ago, I never would have imagined we'd be where we are today. And all because of a video of me. Though the embarrassing footage doesn't show up on my social feed anymore, it still weighs heavy on my mind. Only now I'm not worried about losing my job. I'm worried about losing Sloane.

"It's been so amazing to watch this come together," I tell Sloane quietly. "Thanks for letting me be a part of it."

He squeezes my hand. "This is all you, Hannah."

"What do you think?" Bastien strolls toward us, grinning.

"Everything looks great," Henry says. "Amazing job, once again. Are we still on track for mass production?"

Bastien holds out his hand to Sloane, and they shake, my right hand remaining anchored in Henry's grasp. "Three out of four of our production locations are in place and running. The bulk of the designs will be in stock in time for the launch. That's the best I could do."

"That works," Sloane says. "The deadlines were very tight."

Trista moves to join Bastien, her gaze falling to where Sloane and I remain hand-in-hand. Her eyes flick up to mine, and she smiles knowingly.

"Speaking of deadlines," I interrupt, "when do you think

we'll have today's photos back?"

Bastien glances at the cameraman before looking back at me. "Tomorrow?"

I can't stop my jaw from falling. "Really? That soon?"

The photographer frowns.

"Is that too soon?" I ask him. "In the past, I've had to wait at least a week or more."

He hums. "We can get the files to you tomorrow, but they won't be touched up."

"That works," I tell him. "I can use the untouched versions in my comps and then swap them out for the edited ones when they're ready."

He gives me a thumbs up and my heart races. This is happening. We're doing what I told Sloane was near impossible.

Henry and I say our goodbyes to the team, and I grin at him as we come to a stop outside Bastien's studio. "I jumped the gun earlier. You don't mind if I do the creatives, do you? It shouldn't take long. Seriously, I can mock up some samples in a day to give you the general concept, and we can go from there."

"I love seeing you excited like this." He leans over to kiss my forehead and pulls me into a hug. "You've brought us this far, I wouldn't dare deny you. On one condition," he adds. "Let me take you out on a date. A real one. To celebrate."

Wrapping my arms around him, I tip my head up to kiss his lips. "I'd love that. What night are you thinking?"

"Tomorrow. Come home with me after work. You can get ready at my place and then we'll leave from there. Unless you want me to come and pick you up at your place."

"Oh my god, no." He's never been to my apartment, and I'd like to keep it that way.

He shakes his head, grinning. "I know where you live, Hannah. I don't mind."

I groan. "You'll get mugged or something. And Candy and Crystal will be all over you like the black flies in July."

"Crystal and Candy?"

"The uh… the *working ladies* in front of my building. They're harmless, really. We've had worse, but they will tag team you and have you wishing you'd never stopped in front of my apartment.

"This is New York, Hannah. Prostitutes are everywhere, even on the Upper East Side."

I sigh. "I know. Please, just don't. It's embarrassing. It's a dumpy area—you would be appalled. You can take me home with you after work."

He grins. "I like the sound of that. We'll shower together. Save water."

I laugh. "That's what Vi and Tessa always say. We both know it doesn't save time *or* water."

He shrugs. "Yeah, but we can pretend."

"We don't need an excuse to shower together." I kiss his lips again.

"You're right," he says between kisses. "Shower-fuck then dinner."

CHAPTER *twelve*

Sloane is acting different, but I'm not sure *why*. I can't quite put my finger on it.

He's sweeter somehow.

Softer.

Very unlike his usual no-nonsense self. I've seen his playful side, and it's delightful, but this is something else entirely.

On the elevator ride up to his penthouse suite, he entwines his fingers with mine and smiles down at me. "You hardly left your desk today. Did you find time to stop for lunch?"

I shake my head. "I ate, don't worry." Only an apple though, because I spent the better part of my day glued to my desk, plugging away at designs for the 212 campaign. It's vital that when combined, each piece of artwork creates a cohesive look similar to Sloane's corporate brand but also unique to the women's line. I think I achieved that. "Did you see the photos

Bastien's team sent over?"

"I haven't. Will they work for what you have in mind?"

I fight to keep my excitement contained. "Yes. Definitely. Oh, Henry, they're perfect. I got so much done today, I can hardly believe it. The comps are done for social and print. I even finished a rough draft of the brand guidelines."

"Good." He brings my hand up to his lips and kisses my fingers. "But enough about work. It's Friday. Date night."

"That's right." I bite my lip to keep my smile at bay. "Shower-fuck then dinner."

He shrugs.

"No shower-fuck?" I pout. "Is everything okay?"

The elevator doors slide open to the entrance of his suite, and he tugs me gently until I follow him. "Everything is good. Better than good." He squeezes my hand. "You make me happy, Hannah."

There's no stopping the aww that slips from my mouth. "You make me happy, too."

Sloane leads me to his living room and gestures for me to sit. After several trips to his kitchen, the coffee table between the sofas is covered in small platters of cheese and crackers and assorted fruits.

He hands me a glass of wine, the weighty look in his eyes making me nervous. "Are you hungry? Please, eat."

I shake my head, my mind reeling with concern. Something's up. "I'm fine. What going on, Henry? You're acting... different. I'm here if you need to talk. Or vent, or whatever."

Sloane shifts on the couch, angling himself toward me so we're sitting knee-to-knee. "This is more than just sex to me."

My stomach hurtles to my throat. Does he think I only want him for sex? I mean, sure, we fuck a lot—an exorbitant amount —but there's so much more I love about him. He's smart. And funny. And considerate. A true gentleman in every way, even if he's filthy in the bedroom. "It's more than just sex for me too," I tell him. "I hope you don't think I only want you for your body."

"I don't." He leans in and kisses me softly on the mouth. "I want to make sure you know how much you mean to me. Even I can admit, I'm a little rusty at this romance stuff. It's been years since I've been in a serious relationship."

Not since Eleanor, I add in my head. I don't like that woman. She was wrong for him in every way. I'm so glad she's gone.

"I'm a slave to my job," he continues. "Always have been. But lately, I find myself watching the clock and counting the hours until I can be alone with you. You beguile me."

His bright blue eyes bore into me as he smiles, and butterflies attack my gut. He's much better at this *romance stuff* than he gives himself credit for.

I set my hand on his thigh. "You're much sweeter than you realize."

He grins. "I'm glad you think so. Now, eat. I'll be right back." Sloane jumps off the couch and disappears down the hallway. When he returns a few minutes later, he pulls me up into his embrace. His lips find mine, his fingers snaking up underneath my blouse. "I could do nothing but kiss you, and I'd die a happy man," he says into my ear. "But come with me." He leads me down the hallway toward his bedroom.

"I know where this is going," I joke. Except when I step into his room, I lose my breath. He's drawn the curtains and dimmed the lights. Around the room, candles coat every surface, and a vase of gorgeous flowers sits on the nightstand next to the side of the bed where I usually sleep. "Sloane…"

"There's more." He gently nudges me farther into the room and takes me to his master ensuite. The aroma of vanilla, lavender and strawberry mingles in the air along with a soothing piano melody. The large jacuzzi tub in the corner is nearly overflowing with bubbles, and candles light the space. It's beautiful. And romantic. And such a sweet, sweet gesture.

"You did all this for me?"

Sloane turns me to face him and tips my chin up so I can look at him. "Do you like it?" He smiles when I nod and passes me one of the hair ties I keep in his bathroom drawer.

"You thought of everything, didn't you?" I say, reaching behind my head to tie up my hair.

He works at the buttons on my blouse and strips me out of my clothes until I'm standing naked in front of him. "I've thought of nothing but this all day."

"Now you," I breathe, working clumsily at his buttons.

With his dress shirt open, I run my palms over his chest and push the fabric off his shoulders.

He hums.

"And your pants." I kneel on the floor as I strip him naked.

Other than our quiet breaths and the soft piano melody, the room is silent. The air is filled with something different today. The urgency is absent, but it hasn't diminished our need to connect. It's made it stronger.

Henry steps into the bath, extending his hand to help me in. Sitting with my back to his front, I lie cocooned between his legs, his arms around me, smoothing over my skin.

My nipples harden to tiny buds, and I lay my head on his chest. Need overflows from every sensitive pore. I want his hands on every part of me. I need a release, but what we're sharing is so much more profound. It'll be a long, drawn-out affair of the most wonderful kind, and well worth the wait.

"I could lie here forever," he says in my ear. "Shut the world out and not worry about anything but you and me." His fingers slip between my folds. "Right, Hannah? Wouldn't that be nice?"

I hum an agreeable sound that's close to an mm-hmm, and his fingers rub slow circles over my clit.

"That feel good?" he asks, his voice low and gritty in my ear.

The sweetest torture imaginable. "So good," I breathe.

His fingers slow as my back begins to arch.

"Not yet. I want you in my bed. I want you bare today. No more condoms."

My pussy clenches. We had *the talk* last week, the I'm-clean-and-on-the-pill, what-about-you speech. He'd cracked a joke about also being clean but not on the pill, and that conversation morphed into another fuck-fest on the living room floor. With a condom. He wasn't ready, and I was okay with that.

Sloane dries me off with a soft, white towel before scooping me into his arms. I won't ever tire of this. The feeling of being featherlight in his arms.

He deposits me in the middle of his bed and crawls between my legs, hovering over me. "I'm falling in love with you, Hannah. I'm powerless to stop it."

My heart hammers against my chest. *Henry Sloane loves*

me. I pull his head down to mine and kiss his lips. "Before you, I thought I knew what love was, but that's nothing compared to what I feel for you. You've ruined me in the best possible way."

Henry captures my mouth, and in one slow movement, he pushes inside me. We moan together, a harmonious, low melody. Clutching at his shoulders, I wrap my legs around his waist and lock my ankles behind his back. It changes the angle, and now every slow thrust rubs me just where I need it. I moan again, louder this time, less harmonious and more raw. I want to last, I want to hold out for him until he's ready, but my body won't listen to my brain.

"I can't," I pant. "I'm close."

Changing the pace, Sloane, pushes inside me, over and over in short, hard strokes. "Now," he grits, slamming into me. "Come for me, Hannah."

I shatter around him, my nails digging into his shoulders, my back arching off the bed.

His release catches me off guard, a loud, raw growl that pushes me over the edge again. I pulse around him as he stays buried, his cock inside me, his head in the crook of my neck.

"Oh god, Hannah, what you do to me. Fuck, you make me crazy, you know that?"

I grin against his neck. "I hope I make you half as crazy as you make me."

Sloane lifts his head and finds my gaze. "I was wrong about what I said earlier. I'm not falling in love with you." He nips my bottom lip with his teeth. "I'm already there. I love you, Hannah. You own my heart."

***

The restaurant Henry picked out for our first official date is perfect. A steakhouse in the heart of Manhattan, nothing so fancy that I feel out of place, but still upscale.

Throughout dinner, we talk about anything and everything. There's nothing off-limits with him, and I love that. He's an open book.

By the time we're finished our main course, I've gushed way too much about the new campaign, but we've nailed down lots of the little details I needed to talk to him about for the 212 after-launch party.

"As of this morning, we're booked for the Plaza Hotel," I tell him.

His brow furrows. "How'd you manage that? Last I'd heard they were booked a year out."

I grin. "A little begging. A lot of luck."

"Cancellation?"

"Yep. I was calling to find out about getting on the waitlist, and the lady had just gotten off the phone with a bride calling off her wedding."

"Aw, too bad."

"Worked out well for us, though," I chuckle.

"Oooh, you're ruthless, Hannah. I love it."

"I know, right?" I laugh. "And we can use the Plaza's caterers and decorators if we want. That will save a lot of time and hassle."

"Let's do it. What else?"

I blow out a puff of air. "Ugh. So much. I have a master spreadsheet plotted out with all the details. Maybe we can meet next week and firm things up?"

"Anytime, you want." Reaching across the table, Sloane takes my hand. "Did I tell you you've made quite the impression at work?"

I raise my brow. "Oh?"

He nods. "Your name came up at the quarterly meeting. Hudson Roth said he needs someone like you on his team. A go-getter to up his game. We have a friendly rivalry."

"Of course, you do," I smile. Boys.

"He's always trying to one-up me, so I sometimes remind him that technically, he works for his mom. And then he reminds me that he made his first million at sixteen, a year earlier than me—so he claims."

I scoff, "Yeah, well, when *I* was sixteen, I had a lucrative dog-walking business that netted me twenty bucks a week."

He laughs. "You're an entrepreneur at heart."

I shake my head. "Not quite. I spent more time designing posters and trying out different marketing strategies than I did actually walking the dogs. Plus, my concept was flawed."

"Why's that?"

My phone buzzes in my purse, but I ignore it. "I only catered to the one percent."

His brow quirks up at my playful poke, and I give him a cheeky smile. "It's true, though. My customer base was tiny. I only walked dogs who lived within a two-mile radius of my house. And they had to be puppies."

"Puppies? So what happened when they weren't puppies anymore?"

I laugh under my breath. "Well, the whole thing sort of fizzled out. Puppies are a handful. After that, my mom started her own business, so I worked for her when I wanted extra money."

"The same holistic business she owns now?"

I nod. "She's always been into the hippie-dippie stuff." My phone vibrates again, but this time, I pull it out to check it.

I've missed a bunch of texts from Davis and three from Vi. Instinctively, my eyes flick up to check the time. Seven twenty-two. Shit.

My pulse sprints to catch up to my racing heart as I skim the messages from Davis.

It's D-Day.

Tick tock, Hannah Banana.

Cutting it close this week...

Ignoring me won't make me go away.

Beep. Time's up.

I frown. That's it? No threat to send it to Sloane? Could he have been bluffing all along?

Circling back, I tap on Vi's name.

Hey! Call me. I've got AMAZING news!

Hannah?

Get off Sloane's dick and pick up, dammit!

I peek up at Sloane. "I'm so sorry, Vi's been trying to get a hold of me. I need to call her, okay?"

He smiles at me sweetly. "Take your time, love."

Awww. *Love.* Oh, god. I could listen to him call me that all day. "I'll be quick, I promise." Pushing away from the table, I walk toward the entrance of the restaurant and tap on Vi's name.

She picks up straight away. "Finally! We've got the money, Hannah! We did it!"

"What?" I turn away from the people gawking at me and lower my voice. "How?"

"You won't believe it," she says. "Tessa and I were outside bitching about you needing a measly four hundred dollars, and

Candy and Crystal overheard us. They offered to front the money."

"For real? In exchange for what? Why would they do that?"

"Because they said we're nice. And apparently, you often give money to Gus."

I do. Mostly in the winter or if I have spare change weighing down my purse, but still. "Are you serious? That's amazing."

"I just went to the bank and transferred it to you. It should be in your account already."

"Oh my god, thank you, Vi. You guys are amazing. I owe you."

"Text Davis," she yells. "Hurry. Before he does something stupid."

"I'm going to, right now." I hang up on Vi and rapid-fire a bunch of messages to Davis.

I have your money.

I'm sorry it's late.

I'm sending it now.

When he doesn't respond, I jump over to my banking app and transfer the money. I tap out another message as quickly as I can, cursing my fingers when they keep hitting the wrong letters.

It's sent.

I stare at the screen, praying for a quick response. Answer me, dammit.

Dots tumble along the bottom of the screen.

I hold my breath.

Too late.

No! My heartbeat stumbles to a halt as his messages continue to pour in.

Sloane already agreed to my price.

That man has deep pockets.

Should be getting that file any second now.

Yup.

Delivered.

No!

My pulse whooshes in my ears as I suck in breath after staggered breath. My body breaks into an instant sweat. I'm too late.

I hang my head, my body trembling with pent-up shame. I should have told him. Maybe not at first, but as soon as we grew closer, he deserved to know.

Weaving around the tables, I make my way toward him as fast as I can without drawing attention. He stares at his phone, pinching at the screen to zoom in.

"Wait." The desperate whisper slips from my mouth though he's too far away to hear me.

His brows draw together.

Seconds tick by like minutes as I fight the urge to run to him and take his phone. Let me be the one to tell him.

His eyes grow wide.

It's me. I'm sorry.

His shoulders drop, his expression morphing from confusion to shock to anger before settling on something that obliterates my aching heart: Indifference.

"I can explain," I say, clutching onto the back of my chair to keep myself from crumbling. Drawing one slow breath after another, I wait for him to acknowledge my presence. "Henry?"

"I don't want to hear your lies." He stands from his chair and tosses a bunch of fifties on the table without meeting my gaze. Pulling another fifty from his pocket, he throws the bill onto my empty plate. "Take a cab home. I can't even look at you right now."

CHAPTER thirteen

Disobeying Sloane's instructions, I leave his fifty on the table and take the subway home. His words circle through my head in an endless loop until I burst through our apartment door in tears.

I can't even look at you right now.

With no one home to hear me, I cry loud, ugly sobs into my pillow until darkness falls and my tears run dry. Sometime later, footfalls in my bedroom stir me from my troubled sleep.

"I told you we should have come home earlier," Tessa whispers, turning on the bedside lamp.

"I didn't know," Vi hisses. "I thought it was all good. We got the money."

Tessa sits on the edge of my bed as I lay curled in the fetal position. "Sweetie, what happened?" She pushes my hair away from my face and grimaces. "Oh, honey."

I throw my arm over my eyes and groan. "Don't. I'm fine."

"I'll get a cloth." Vi disappears from my room before returning with a warm, wet towel.

Like a true friend, Tessa wipes the makeup from my face while Vi sits on the other side of me and rubs my back. "Talk to us. What can we do?"

Take me back in time. Back before Sloane. Back before heartache.

I tell them everything, my body shuddering as I recount the good and the goddamn awful. "I love him. I hate that I hurt him."

"You're not alone, Hannah. I'd have done the same thing," Vi says.

Tessa nods. "Me too. He can't blame you for not wanting to lose your job."

"I don't know if I even have a job to go back to on Monday. You have no idea how many times he talked about the *damn girl in the video* and how much trouble she caused him. I had so many chances to speak up." I sniffle. "But I didn't."

"If he can't see that you were between a rock and a hard place, well, that's on him."

We sit in silence until Tessa yawns, setting off a chain reaction with Vi and me.

"I'm sorry," I tell them. "It's late. I'll be fine."

Two sets of worried eyes study my face. "Let us know if you need anything, Hannah," Vi says.

I nod. "I will. Don't let me sulk too long. And keep me out of the ice cream, okay?"

***

True to their word, Tessa and Vi cater to my sombre mood

for about three hours Saturday morning. It's noon when Tessa's finally had enough. "Give me that." She takes my quart of cookie dough ice cream and tsks. "A pint wouldn't do? Where did you even find this?"

I hold up my phone. "I had it delivered after I read through the messages I sent to Sloane last night. We're definitely done, and I'm going to be unemployed, I know it. Listen to this." I read out the list of desperate messages I sent at four a.m. when my body refused to let me sleep. "Oh, here's my favorite. This is so classy... Please don't fire me. I need the money. I owe my friends money. I even owe the hookers out front four hundred big ones."

Vi and Tess groan in unison.

"I mean this in the nicest possible way," Tessa starts, "but were you drunk?"

I shake my head. "No. Just tired—and apparently delirious. Can I please have my ice cream back?"

Vi nods at Tessa. "Yeah, give it back." She points toward the kitchen. "I'll grab two more spoons."

***

Having not heard otherwise, I return to work on Monday morning fully prepared to be fired. I'm fussing with the positioning of #ThisIsMe on a social ad when a new meeting notification pops up on my screen—a ten o'clock team meeting in Sloane's office. I blow out a breath. I've been on tenterhooks since I arrived, waiting for the inevitable. But perhaps I was wrong. Maybe my job *is* safe—at least until the end of my contract.

I print out my notes and make sure my spreadsheet is up-to-date before heading to Sloane's office ten minutes early. If he's alone, I want to have a private word. I owe him an apology. Multiple apologies, starting with the video and ending with the ambush of text messages I sent the other night.

Outside his office, Pam's on the phone, but she gestures for me to go ahead.

I knock quietly before entering, just to be safe. Behind his desk, Sloane types on his keyboard. He glances up at me when I walk in but returns to whatever he's working on and pretends he didn't see me.

Clearing my throat, I step toward his desk and square my shoulders, trying to project confidence. I don't want him thinking I'm as meek and pathetic as I made myself sound in those late-night texts. "Henry—"

"No." He takes off his reading glasses and drops them on his desk. "*Not* Henry. *Not* Sloane. *Mr.* Sloane."

My shoulders slump. I know he's angry. He has every right to be, but I'd hoped we could have a mature conversation. Apparently not.

At the oval table, I choose a spot at the opposite end from where Henry usually sits and sort through my printouts. Inevitably, my wayward thoughts drift back to the evening we stayed late and fucked on this table, me bent over the edge while Sloane took me hard and fast from behind. It had been the first of many late nights spent in his office, mostly brainstorming and bantering. Words always came easy to us, and time seemed to slip away without warning.

I shake away the memory.

Even now, my head can't reconcile with my heart. I ache to tell him about the inconsequential details of my morning. How I spoke to Crystal and Candy outside my building for the first time today. How Crystal cracked a joke that made me laugh. And how even though their jobs are morally questionable, I can appreciate that they're regular people trying to make it in the big, bad world like the rest of us.

It's awkward sitting in Sloane's office while he ignores me from behind his desk. I'm about to take a second stab at breaking the silence when Pam knocks. She takes the empty spot beside me, and I make small talk with her until Bastien and Gerald arrive as well. It's not until we're all seated that Sloane joins us at the head of the table.

His direction is swift and precise. He wants updates from each of us on where we stand with the 212 product launch. Bastien's update is brief since he spoke to Sloane on Friday about production. He passes a paper to each of us with exact numbers and timelines and a list of which products may not meet the deadline.

Sloane scowls, clearly in a foul mood. "Is there any way we can get a few more of these pieces in the store before the first?"

Bastien shakes his head. "Only if you want to compromise quality. It's too late in the game to find another supplier."

"Fair enough," Sloane says. "Ms. O'Keefe, you're next. I want a full update to make sure everyone is in the loop. Where are you with the designs, the after-party, et cetera?"

My heart lurches at his formal use of my name, but I manage to recover. I glance around the table, avoiding his glare. "I've mocked up many of the designs using the photos Bastien's team sent over Friday morning." I meet Bastien's gaze. "Please thank your photographer. The photos are really wonderful."

Sloane whisks his hand in a *move-along* motion. "Keep it brief."

"I'm sorry." I take a moment to regroup, skimming my notes to see where I left off. "Um, as I said, the concepts are there. Once the final photos arrive, they need to be swapped out before the files are sent to the printer or scheduled on social channels. I've received confirmation from the Plaza that we're a go for the first of July. There was a cancellation," I add.

A quiet huff from Sloane's side of the table has me glancing that way. "We don't need to know why, Ms. O'Keefe. Keep it moving."

I ball my fists under the table and fight to stay upbeat. "I brought notes on everything I've mentioned, as well as my master spreadsheet with all of the details for the after-party. That's the main priority now. I'd love to get some feedback on my ideas if we have time. Oh—I almost forgot. I brought some samples of what I've come up with so far." I lay several designs on the table.

"Wow!" Pam slides one of the papers toward her. "These are fantastic!"

Gerald nods. "Very nice, Hannah."

"Oui, très bien," Bastien agrees.

I can't help but grin. I'm so proud of these designs. "Thanks, guys."

"I don't like them," Sloane grumbles. "They're not what I had in mind."

"What *did* you have in mind?" I whip my head around to Sloane. He's being difficult for the sake of it. "I tried to keep the designs similar to the feel of the men's line but with an added feminine touch. Together, it creates cohesion between both lines of clothing while still reflecting the tastes of each audience. I've laid it all out in the brand guidelines." I pass around copies of the draft document. "There are still a few gaps to fill in, but this will give you a general idea."

Sloane shakes his head, obviously not pleased. "Nobody asked you to do this."

"I-I know," I stammer. "It's a standard document in the design industry. I'm sure there was one created for your men's line, Mr. Sloane."

"No. There wasn't. Anything else?"

I rack my brain, skimming my notes a second time. "That's all I can think of at the moment."

"Fine. Pam, anything else you need to know?"

Pam looks up from where she's scribbling furiously on her notepad. "I think I'm good. Has anything else been booked for the 212 after-launch party?"

I shake my head. "Only the Plaza. Everything else is up in the air. I've added a list of potential vendors beside each idea in the spreadsheet. This afternoon I'll—"

"It's fine," Sloane interrupts. "Ger? What about you?"

Gerald pushes his glasses up the bridge of his nose. "No concerns." He smiles at me from across the table, and I try my best to return an equally genuine grin. It probably falls flat, but he doesn't seem to notice.

Closing his notebook, Sloane sets his pen on top. "Thank you. Pam will send along the minutes as soon as they're ready. Bastien, I'll touch base in about a week for an update."

Bastien, Pam and Gerald stand to leave, and I work quickly to gather the papers I'd spread across the table.

"Ms. O'Keefe, stay a moment. I need a word." Sloane moves to his desk and sits in his big leather chair.

Great. Now what? Is it possible he's going to apologize for

acting like an ass? Unlikely.

His intercom buzzes. "Mr. Sloane, Sandra is here, should I send her in?"

"Thank you, Pam. Please do."

Sandra? HR Sandra? My insides twist into a mangled mess of knots. I should have known. He wanted all the details so he could pass my project on to someone else—because I'm fired.

When Sandra pushes through his office door, Henry comes back to the table and gestures for her to join us. "Good morning. I'm sorry to throw all of this at you on such short notice."

She smiles at him like a woman with a crush on the pool boy. "My pleasure, Mr. Sloane." She turns to me, her smile less warm, yet still professional. "Hannah, how are you? How was your trip to California?"

My fingers play at the pile of papers in front of me, unsure of whether she knows what I said was a lie. "Actually, I didn't end up going after all."

"Aww, that's too bad, dear." She looks genuinely disappointed.

Sloane clears his throat and gestures to the documents Sandra brought in with her. "Shall we get started?"

"Of course." She hands me several documents, all held in place with a bright blue paper clip that matches the color of Sloane's eyes.

I skim the printout. The first few words I land on are non-negotiable, Hudson Roth, and immediately.

"So, as you can see," Sandra says, "this contract—"

Sloane holds up his hand. "I've got this."

She nods.

He turns to face me, his eyes more dark and stormy than the

beautiful blue I remember. "Your services are no longer needed in my division. In the interest of honoring your contract, I've arranged for you to assist Mr. Roth for the remainder of the agreement."

Eleanor's face flashes through my mind. What was it that Trista said about Sloane moving her to another division? It was a *win-win* because he wouldn't have to see her? And now he doesn't want to see me, so he's getting rid of me, too?

I hang my head, pretending to review the contract. Beneath the table, my nails dig craters into my palms to keep my tears in check. I won't give him the pleasure of seeing me cry.

"Eva Roth is one of the founders of ERS Inc., best known for her involvement in the real estate industry," Sandra cites. "Under her son, Hudson Roth, you'll assist his team with marketing various properties in his portfolio." She flips to the second page. "Your pay will remain the same, and the rest of the contract is identical to the previous one. Should you choose to sign, I'll take you upstairs straight away and get you settled in."

"And if I don't?" I try to meet Henry's gaze, but his eyes remain locked on the contract.

"You'll no longer be employed by Evans, Roth and Sloane," Sandra says, her tone unwavering.

I glance at Sloane a second time, but the paper still holds his interest.

I can't even look at you right now.

He wants me gone, but I've guilted him into making me someone else's problem.

"Take a few minutes to read it over," Sandra offers.

"I've already made my decision." I push the paper away from me, withdrawing my hands before Henry can see them shaking.

A flicker of surprise crosses his face before it disappears behind his mask.

"Are you sure?" she asks.

I throw away my future with a single nod. "Thank you for this opportunity, Mr. Sloane," I say, my voice barely above a whisper.

Forcing myself to stand, I leave my notes, my pen, and my heart on the table. "I won't ever forget it." I won't ever forget *you.*

CHAPTER *fourteen*

I'm two steps away from the safety of the elevator when Sandra calls out to me.

"Hannah! Not so fast. I'm too old to chase you." Her heels click-clack on the floor as she catches up to me. "You can't leave just yet," she puffs.

I stare at her unblinking. There's nothing important at my desk, certainly nothing important enough worth braving the looks on the faces of all my colleagues.

"Paperwork." Sandra grabs onto my arm and sucks in another ragged breath.

"Are you all right?" I ask her, genuinely concerned.

She nods, drawing several deep breaths in a row. "I'm not as spry as I once was." She straightens herself, adjusting her blouse and twisting her pearl necklace back into place. "Before you leave—and please, I hope you will reconsider—I need to you sign some forms."

My shoulders drop. I just want to get out of here. I want to be home in my bed with a big bowl of ice cream while Tessa and Vi aren't awake to steal it.

On the other hand, getting everything done now means I don't need to come back another time and risk running into *Mr.* Sloane. "I guess I can sign them now. How long do you need?"

"I'll be quick," she says, no longer winded. She's back to her polished self, and no one but me is any the wiser.

"Sandra?" I work my bottom lip between my teeth and swallow my pride. No more lies. "While I'm here, would it be possible to get a check for last week instead of waiting until Friday's pay? I'm… a little short on cash right now."

Sandra eyes me carefully as if weighing her options. It's worth a shot. I'd rather not owe Crystal and Candy any money no matter how nice they seem. For all I know, it could belong to their pimp, and they might send him my way to collect it.

"I understand if doing it all manually is too much trouble. I just thought I'd ask," I add.

Sandra looks past me.

"Cut her a check, Sandra."

I drop my head. Fucking Sloane.

"Yes, sir." She smiles at me, a gentle sort of grin that's almost motherly. "I need about ten minutes, dear, and then I'll go over everything with you."

"Thank you. I appreciate it."

Sandra's barely in her office before Sloane is at my side. "What the fuck, Hannah?" he whisper-yells.

"I should be asking you the same thing," I hiss, crossing my arms over my chest. "I am *not* Eleanor."

Sloane glances at the row of cubicles along the wall before grabbing my arm and pulling me into one of the dark meeting rooms near Sandra's office. Sensing our movement, the lights flicker on. He whips the door closed without letting it slam and turns to face me. "What are you talking about?"

"That contract." I step toward him, my earlier humiliation escalating to rage. "You think I can't tell what you're trying to do?"

Standing his ground, he stays rooted in place, so close I can hear him breathe. The air is charged between us, the tension a heady mix of fury and pheromones. "What are you talking about? I offered you a better job that could jumpstart your career, and you threw it back in my face."

"I did not! You want me gone—just like Eleanor. She pissed you off and you sent her away. Made it look like a promotion."

He shakes his head, opening his mouth as if to speak, but I cut him off. I'm not done. Nowhere close.

"That's right. I know all about what you did. And you know, maybe *she* deserved it—but *I* don't. I put my heart and soul into this campaign. My heart and *fucking soul.*" I poke him in the chest as I emphasize my words. "If you think I didn't have your best interest in mind, you're wrong. Because I did. *Always.*" My voice cracks on the last word. I try to push my pain aside, but it's no use. "That video of me—it was humiliating. The comments people wrote—they were awful. Soul-crushing."

"Hannah, stop." The gritty sound of my name on his lips does nothing to slow me down. I couldn't stop now if I wanted to.

"You want to know what's sad? I used to like my body. My curves. I was good with all of it. That fucking video stole *everything* from me. My confidence. My job. My… *You.*" I suck in a shuddery breath and reach for the door handle. I've said too much.

Sloane reaches for it too, but I stop him with my palm on his chest. "No. I'm leaving. Sandra can mail the check. The paperwork too."

I meet his stare, pleading with my eyes for him to let me go. My lower lip quivers, my resolve wavering. "*Please.*"

He steps back, saying nothing, and I leave the room without looking back.

***

By the time Tessa and Vi wake up at four in the afternoon to get ready for work, I've wallowed through the stages of grief with a pint of vanilla and exorbitant amounts of chocolate sauce.

"Oh, god, not again," Tessa says when she finds me in the living room.

"Did he fire you?" Vi says, appalled. She moves the throw cushion aside and sits next to me on the couch. "I'll go kick his ass for you. Right now. I think I could take him."

Tessa's eyebrow quirks, and I hold back my smile. Vi's no threat to a fly. She couldn't kick anyone's ass, even if she wanted to.

"It's the thought that counts," Tessa quips, reading my thoughts. "But seriously, what happened?"

"I quit."

They screech their whats and whys in unison followed by a rapid-fire exchange of questions.

For the next few minutes, I recount my horrid morning. "It's fine. I'm over it. I'm over Sloane."

"Mm-hmm," Tessa says, unconvinced. "Sure, you are."

"I am!"

Two loud knocks rattle our apartment door, and the three of us freeze.

"Hannah, I know you're in there."

My eyes grow wide, and I mouth the word *Sloane*.

He knocks again.

Tessa creeps to the door and peers through the peephole before looking back at us. "It's him," she whispers.

"I can hear you," his voice says beyond the door.

My head lolls back. Fuck my life.

"Let me handle this." Vi shoos Tessa out of the way and opens the door as far as the chain lock will allow. "What do you want, Sloane—I mean, *Mr. Sloane*?"

"I have a check for Hannah. May I speak with her, please?"

"No."

"Are you Violet? Hannah's told me lots about you."

"So what if I am?"

Tessa nudges her out of the way.

"Tessa, hello."

"Don't *hello* me, Sloane. Hannah doesn't want to see you. You're wasting your time. She's over you."

"*Way* over you," Vi adds.

Tessa shoves her hand through the tiny gap in the door. "I'll take her check and make sure she gets it."

Even from where I'm sitting, I hear the heaviness in Henry's sigh. Tessa takes the check and closes the door harder than necessary. My insides twist. They're just trying to protect me, but a tiny piece of me hates how they're being mean to him.

"Ugh. He's way too pretty when he's sad like that." Vi says, coming back to sit with me.

"He looked sad?" I move to stand from the couch, but Tessa stops me.

"He's gone. Here, he brought your check."

Slipping my finger under the flap of the envelope, I tear it open. "That's not right." It's much more than six days' pay. "It's way too much."

"Just cash it," Tessa says. "It's pennies to him."

"True." My heart sinks at a reminder of the difference in our social status. "I'll put it in the bank tomorrow."

***

I spend the better part of the following morning on the computer applying for jobs across New York City before cashing the check from Sloane at the bank. Four hundred dollars in hand, I look for Crystal and Candy to pay them back, but they're not hanging around out front. I'll have to try and find them later.

On my way back to our apartment, my cell phone rings. I dig it out of my purse as I climb the stairs but tap the ignore button when I don't recognize the number.

Pick up.

The anonymous text lights up my screen before the phone rings again.

"Hello?"

"Hannah Banana, hello. How are you?"

Pressing the phone to my ear, I strain to hear the vaguely familiar voice. "Davis?"

He hums his affirmation with a creepy satisfaction that makes me shiver.

I speed up my pace. "You've got some nerve calling me."

"I wanted to check in on you. Rumor has it, you have a broken heart."

The contents of my stomach curdle. He knows about Sloane.

"Do you still work for him?"

"No." Stabbing my key into the lock, I fiddle with it until it unlocks and dart inside.

He hums again. "I bet you're pissed."

"I'm over it," I say, twisting the deadbolt into place.

"You and I both know that's bullshit."

"I'm hanging up now." I slide the chain lock through the groove. I'm not taking any chances.

"Wait. I have something for you."

Goosebumps race up my arms. I move to the window and peek between the slats of the blinds. "Stay away from me, Davis."

"You'll like this, Hannah, I promise."

My phone dings with an incoming text.

"Watch it. You'll see what I mean."

Putting Davis on speakerphone, I switch to my messaging app and press the play button on the video thumbnail.

I gasp.

Surveillance footage.

Of Sloane.

He stands in front of my apartment building with Crystal and Candy, pointing to his car before Candy nods. The video loses focus, but when it clears, Sloane is handing the two of them money. A lot of it.

I play the clip again.

"Oh my god," I whisper. The evidence is damning, but I know exactly what this is. Sloane paid Candy and Crystal the four hundred dollars I owed them. I open my mouth to defend Sloane but Davis interrupts me.

"That's right, Hannah. You and I have both been wronged by Sloane."

My head whirs with jumbled thoughts. Davis has a beef with Sloane? Why? "How did you get this?" We don't have security that I'm aware, so it must be from a neighboring building.

"What matters is what we do with it."

We? Jesus. Davis is crazy. I shouldn't be engaging. But at the same time, if he has plans to hurt Sloane, I need details. I need to play along. "What do you have in mind? I might be game."

The line goes quiet.

"Are you still there?" I pace the living room. This is so fucked up.

"I don't know that I can trust you."

"Henry Sloane is a dick," I tell him, injecting my voice with added vexation. "No one hates him more than me. And for the record, he didn't fire me. I quit."

"Interesting."

"So?"

He makes that skeevy humming noise again. "How about this? If you help me, I'll give you your money back. All of it."

"What if we get caught?" I ask, trying to sound convincingly worried.

"We won't. I have it all planned out. We're going to ruin him." Davis rambles on, growing more and more excited the longer he goes on about his plan.

He's delusional.

But worse than that, I'm afraid his plan might work.

CHAPTER *fifteen*

Davis's plan could ruin Sloane in every possible way. Personally. Professionally. His brand. His reputation. His livelihood.

And as mad as I am at him for trying to slough me off to Hudson Roth, I can't let that happen.

Rather than call the cops and chance Davis seeing them on whatever security footage he's tapped into, I take a taxi to the nearest police station.

Taking a number from the dispenser, I linger near the information desk until it's finally my turn.

"I need to speak to an officer, please," I tell the woman at the desk.

"Name, please?"

"Hannah O'Keefe."

"How can we help you today, Hannah?" She peers up at me,

her pen ready to fill out the paper in front of her.

Oh god, where do I start? "I have information about someone planning to defraud Henry Sloane. Davis—I don't know his last name—has video footage of Sloane paying a hooker in front of my apartment, but it's not real. I mean…it *is* real, but it's not what it looks like. Candy loaned me four hundred dollars, and he was paying her back on my behalf." Oh god, that sounds even crazier when I say it out loud.

The officer studies me carefully.

"I swear, I'm not a lunatic—" I glance at the name tag on her desk "—Wanda. I'm telling the truth. Davis blackmailed me for ten thousand dollars and Henry Sloane for twenty-five."

Wanda's brows pull together, her interest piqued.

"I have proof," I tell her, not bothering to hide the desperation in my voice. "Texts. Videos. Phone records— although, those are from an unknown number, but maybe you guys know some trick to decode it or something. I don't know how all that works, I just know I need to try and stop this video from getting out."

"Hannah?"

"Yeah?" I puff.

She smiles sweetly. "Just breathe, honey. Go sit down. I'll find someone for you to talk to."

Relief floods my system, but my heart doesn't slow its pace. It's been racing since my call with Davis. "Okay, thank you. Thank you so much. I really appreciate it."

Wanda points toward a seating area that's cordoned off to one side. I make my way over, my body still trembling, and collapse into the chair. Across from me, a baldheaded man glances up from his phone, and I try not to gasp. His entire face is a mess of weird piercings and tattoos, but it's the snake poised to eat the man's eyeball that creeps me out the most. He smiles at my palpable unease, teeth surprisingly white for a man with a row of piercings along his gum line.

Not wanting to engage, I look away and avoid making eye contact with anyone else. This is New York, and I've seen all walks of life out on the streets, but being this close—even in a police station— puts me on edge.

About ten minutes later, an officer calls me over to a private area, and introduces himself as Officer Francis. I repeat my story, this time with more coherence, and tell him Davis's plan.

"He's going to release the video to the media during Henry Sloane's new product launch. It will humiliate Henry in front of the crowd, the press. You can't be accused of hiring hookers and come back from that. That sort of thing doesn't just blow over when the next scandal goes viral."

Officer Francis scribbles in his notebook, nodding as I give him as many details as I can. "Can I see the video?"

I nod. "It's here on my phone. Everything is. I have the texts. I have emails that show all the transfers I made to him." Holding out the device, I press the button and turn it to face him. It shakes in my hand, and the officer takes it from me.

"You did the right thing coming here, Hannah." He plays the video again, studying it closely. "I see. This is clearly security footage."

"He was paying my debt, not paying for their services," I tell him.

He nods, his expression giving nothing away. I can't tell if he believes me.

"May I take your phone for a moment? I'd like to give it to

our tech team to make copies of this footage, as well as your texts and emails."

"That's fine." I hold it out to him, but the moment he turns to walk away, my mind flickers with recollection. What else is on my phone that he might see?

My secret obsession with early '90s music? Okay. No big deal. Who doesn't enjoy a little Ace of Base?

Wildly inappropriate texts to Sloane? All right, not great, but I can live with that.

Up-close-and-personal naked pics? Oh fuck. Big deal. BIG fucking deal.

Officer Francis returns about thirty minutes later, but I refuse to look him in the eye.

He hands me back my phone. "Thank you, Hannah. We have everything we need. For now, don't delete anything."

"I won't," I lie, already plotting the demise of my naked pics. "What happens now? Do you think you'll be able to track Davis down?" Henry and I may not be together anymore, but I don't wish him any harm.

"We'll try our best, I assure you." He hands me a business card. "I'll call you if I have any further questions."

"Thank you, officer." I shake his hand, my face heating as I accidentally meet his gaze. "I appreciate your help."

***

With hours to kill before Vi and Tessa wake up to start their day, I take advantage of the beautiful late-June weather and wander the paths of Central Park. Their late-night jobs never posed any inconvenience before, but right now, I could really use their advice. Part of me wants to call Sloane and give him a heads-up about the video, but the other part worries I'm butting in where I don't belong.

When did life get so complicated?

Peering up at the gorgeous buildings in the distance, I scan the windows to see if I can pinpoint which one might be Sloane's. It's impossible. They're too far away and too high up. Even the floor-to-ceiling windows look like glass mosaic squares from here.

At a quarter past six, I sidle into the apartment, drained from the drama of the day, but curious to get Vi and Tessa's opinion on what to do next.

Kicking off my shoes, I head straight for the kitchen and fill my favorite mug with Honey Nut Cheerios and milk. I'm starving. I've never been so glad to be off that stupid low-cal, low-fat, low-carb diet. They ought to call it the low-food diet. I doubt I broke six-hundred calories a day.

"You guys up yet?" I shout from the kitchen. "You won't believe the day I had." Shoving a spoonful of cereal into my mouth, I set off to find them. They can't be far. Our two-bedroom apartment doesn't leave a lot of room to hide. With a little luck, they might even have clothes on today.

I'm hardly through the doorway when I freeze mid-step.

Oh shit.

Sloane is sitting on my couch.

I glance from him to the door before settling back on him. "How did you…why are you…who let you…"

"Hi, Hannah." Sloane's piercing eyes meet mine from across the room, his expression unreadable.

What the hell? I spoon another heap of Cheerios into my mouth to buy myself some time. What's he doing here? And more importantly, who the hell let him in?

As if summoned by my thoughts, Vi and Tessa round the corner of the hallway, arguing in heated whispers.

"Vi let him in," Tessa says matter-of-fact, throwing her girlfriend under the bus.

Vi scowls at Tessa before glancing cautiously at me. "I thought it was you banging 'cause you forgot your keys again." She glances at Sloane. "She does that *all* the time."

He hums as if that surprises him.

"What brings you here, Mr. Sloane?" I ask him sweetly, mentally patting myself on the back. That *Mr.* didn't even sound a little snarky.

He stands from the sofa and strolls toward me. "So, the police came to see me today…"

Vi's eyes round into saucers, and I'm sure mine look the same. I swallow my mouthful of half-chewed cereal, trying not to choke.

"…at my office," he continues. "Caused a bit of a stir."

My lips curl into an O as I peer up at him unblinking. "Shit. I didn't think of that. Oh god, I bet that spread gossip throughout the building. Did you—"

Sloane presses his finger to my lips. "I knew it had to be you."

"Me?"

He lowers his hand. "Who went to the police. They wouldn't tell me."

"I'm sorry." My grip tightens around the handle of my makeshift bowl. "I didn't know what else to do."

He shakes his head. "Stop apologizing. I'm not mad, Hannah. You did the right thing. But I want the full story. Officer Francis asked way more questions than he answered."

"When Davis called, I thought he was going to ask for more money, but now he thinks I'm going to help him ruin the 212 launch with that video. He's not right in the head."

Sloane's brows pull together as he frowns.

"Maybe I should start from the beginning," I tell him.

"What do you mean, *more money*? Did he... did you pay him?"

I step back, holding my mug of soggy Cheerios between us.

"How much?" He closes the space between us.

I swallow the lump in my throat and whisper, "Ten."

"Ten thousand?" His head lolls back, clearly frustrated. "Oh, Hannah. *Why?*"

"You paid him twenty-five!" I burst.

"I actually *have* that kind of money. Jesus."

My mouth snaps shut, and my shoulders fall. I'm well aware of how rich he is. There's no need to rub it in my face.

He sighs. "I didn't mean it like that."

"Look around, Sloane. It's no secret that we're not rolling in it."

"I don't care about that. I just wish you'd come to me."

"And said what? Oh, by the way, that idiot girl in the video was me, and now I'm being blackmailed?"

"If you'd told me, he'd have had nothing to blackmail."

"That is true," Vi says, appearing in the doorway before slapping her palm over her mouth.

My eyes roll skyward.

"Sorry." She backs away. "Tessa and I will be over here not listening if you need us." She wanders back to the living room and sits on the couch before waving for Tessa to join her.

"Let's go somewhere more private," Sloane suggests.

"Here is good." Turning my back to him, I set my cereal on the counter beside the sink to deal with later. Once Sloane is gone.

"Please, Hannah. Talk to me." His voice softens, eating away at my resolve. "Don't shut me out."

I close my eyes, fingertips gripping the edge of the counter. The safer choice is asking him to leave, but my heart has trouble with goodbyes. I turn back to face him. "Just for a second." Against my better judgement, I lead Sloane to my bedroom and close the door behind him.

His masculine frame stands out in the tiny space as he peers around the room at all my stuff. "It's so…"

"Small? Cramped? Crappy?" The words roll off my tongue. Even with my double bed pushed up against the wall, the floor space is limited. One good thing about being poor is that there's no extra money to waste on clutter.

"I was going to say *you*." When he turns to me, his smile is wide and gleaming with mischief. "I half expected a corkboard display of all your cute little spreadsheets."

"Don't do this," I whisper.

His brows pull together, seemingly confused.

"Don't be all sweet and funny and expect me to pretend things haven't changed." I stare at my feet, willing my heart to stop sputtering. "You hurt me, Henry. And I know that all this ultimately rests on my shoulders and maybe I deserve it, but it hurts." I sigh. "A lot."

"I'm hurting, too. When I saw that it was you in the video, I felt like I'd been duped. And by someone I trusted so completely."

The truth in his words cuts me through to my core. I sit on

the edge of my bed, peering up at him, my insides twisting. "I'm so sorry I didn't tell you. I should have. I truly regret it."

"I understand why you didn't."

I wring my fingers in my lap. "It was deceitful."

"You didn't want to lose your job."

"Why are you defending me?"

The mattress dips as he sits beside me. "For the same reason that video hurt so much. Because I love you, Hannah."

I suck in a breath, my gaze locked on his. I couldn't look away even if I wanted to. My pulse races to a gallop at the chance of reconciliation before it crashes back to reality. Just because he loves me doesn't mean he wants me back.

Sloane tucks a strand of hair behind my ear, his thumb sweeping across my cheek. "Come back to ERS."

"It's not that easy," I tell him. "I quit."

"It *is* that easy. You didn't sign the papers. Everything is still at your desk. Come back." The corners of his eyes crinkle when he smiles. "Also, I have a bit of pull there. No one will give you trouble."

Working with Henry's team was unforgettable. If I were smart, I'd be jumping at the chance to expand my experience and work for Hudson Roth, but right now, my career isn't my priority. It's my heart. "I don't want to work for Roth," I tell him quietly.

Sloane shifts on the bed, bringing his face closer to mine. His familiar scent caresses my nose, and my traitorous body drifts closer to draw more in. "I was an idiot for suggesting it. You're too good for him."

"Stop being so agreeable."

He leans in a little more, his voice lowering to a gritty

whisper. "Shut me up with your mouth."

"I shouldn't." But I want to. Desperately.

"Then *I* will." Sloane's lips find mine, and it's futile to resist. I'm on my back on the mattress, moaning into his mouth to take off his pants before the minute is up.

Thirty sweaty minutes later, he kisses me softly before climbing off my bed to find his clothes.

"This doesn't change things," I tell him, rooting around in my sheets for my panties.

Sloane picks them up from the floor and tosses them my way. "I thought we were good?"

I lift a shoulder and let it drop. I'm not committing to anything right now. "I had a weak moment. I just...I need some time to think."

Sloane scrubs his palm across his stubbled jaw. "I'm a stubborn man, Hannah, you know that."

"I know. I love that about you."

He grins.

"But," I continue, "I don't want to rush back into things."

"We'll go slow," he counters.

"You couldn't go slow if I tied cinder blocks to your feet."

"Let me try."

"Let me think about it."

His lips press into a firm line. "Fine. Just so you know, I'm not so good at patience either."

"I know." Shifting to the side of the bed against the wall, I pat the empty spot beside me. "Come sit. I'll tell you everything. Don't distract me this time."

He stacks several pillows against the headboard before settling on the mattress. "I promise to behave." He kisses my cheek. "At least for a little while."

"Thank you." I fight my smile. "All right, where should I start?"

"From the beginning," he tells me. "The day you went to Sloane's on Fifth."

I take a deep breath and nod. "All right. Here goes."

By the time Sloane and I finish talking, my heart, my soul, and my body feel lighter. I can finally breathe. It's all in the open now, no more secrets.

Walking him to the apartment door, we pass Vi and Tessa on the couch. He waves to them, and they grin at him stupidly. The only thing that could make this more embarrassing is if they giggled.

"Just ignore them," I say, glaring at the two of them.

Vi gives me two thumbs up behind Henry's back.

We say our goodbyes outside in the hallway, and he respects my request for space. I need to think. I need to look before I leap and maybe make a spreadsheet. The Pros and Cons of Dating Henry Sloane.

Back inside the apartment, I turn to face Tessa and Vi. The TV is muted, and their eyes are as wide as their smiles.

"So…," Vi says. "You guys are back together, huh?"

I shake my head. "Not exactly."

"What? How?" Vi jolts from the couch and Tessa follows behind her. "But you were in there for so long. We heard you… you know…make up."

I stare at Vi and try my best to appear innocent. "We spent most of the time just talking."

Tessa clears her throat. "We heard you fucking."

God bless her directness.

"Turn out you were right all along," Vi says, grinning. "You *can* hear everything through these walls."

CHAPTER *sixteen*

It's been two weeks since I've seen Sloane, but it feels more like forever.

In hindsight, I should have tried harder to resist him in my bedroom because now I've gone and muddied the water. He's made his intentions clear. He wants to be together. He wants to jump back to where we left off and continue at warp speed. But as fun as that was, the pain of watching him walk away left an imprint on my heart, and now I'm hesitant. What if that happens again six months from now? Is it worth the risk? Is *he* worth the risk?

Against Officer Francis's advice to cease all unnecessary contact in case Davis is watching, Sloane coerces me into helping him with the final details of the 212 after-party. It starts as a small favor—a spreadsheet for one of his reports that he's supposedly having trouble with—and ends with him delivering a laptop via courier.

And now this.

A cell phone.

A text from Sloane already waiting for me.

I miss you.

"He's being heavy-handed again," I tell Vi. "First the laptop, now this."

"It's cute," she counters, peeking over my shoulder at the message. "I like him. He's good for you."

"I'm pretty sure that new homeless guy beside Gus isn't really homeless. I think Sloane hired him to watch our building." Seriously. How many homeless men do you see with perfectly-groomed beards?

"He's worried about you, Hannah. Even Officer Francis said Davis is unstable."

"I guess." Admittedly, I do feel safer knowing someone else is keeping an eye out for anything strange happening outside our building.

"So, don't leave him hanging. Tell him you miss him too."

I stare at the screen, allowing myself to swoon a tiny bit at the cute little heart emoji he added. I really do miss him.

"You're just delaying the inevitable," Violet says, poking me. "Put the poor guy out of his misery."

Working my bottom lip between my teeth, I type and retype my reply before settling on a simple *I miss you, too.*

His next text pops up within seconds.

Did Officer Francis come by to see you yet?

Before I can respond, the phone rings in my hand, lighting up with a photo of Sloane in one of his old ad campaigns—wearing only boxer briefs, of course.

I hold back a laugh and tap the button to accept his call. "Nice pic, Sloane."

"Thought you'd like that," he says, his deep voice rumbling in my ear. "Just making sure you don't forget what I look like."

As if I could. "I won't. And please stop sending me stuff. This phone was completely unnecessary. There's no way Davis is sophisticated enough to have hacked mine."

"I'm not taking any chances with you, Hannah. Actually, that's why I'm calling—I talked to Francis. I don't want you involved in luring Davis at the launch. We'll figure out another way."

"I'm doing it. That video shows you paying a hooker, Henry. You can't explain that away."

"If you get hurt, I'll never forgive myself. The police don't even know who they're looking for," he says. "And even if he's arrested, there's no guarantee the video won't get out anyway."

"We have to try."

"What if it's a setup?"

"I don't think it is," I tell him. "I've talked to Davis twice this week already. Every time he calls, he's increasingly brazen. He really thinks he's got you this time. Is it possible you know him? Do you have any enemies?"

He scoffs. "Plenty. It's the nature of my business. But they're a different sort of opponent. We battle it out on the stock market. On the golf course. Or by outbidding each other at a charity event. It's a money game. No, this is something else entirely."

"I guess that's reassuring—" Three knocks sound on the apartment door. "—Hold on a sec, someone's here."

Vi moves toward the door and peers through the peephole

before letting Officer Francis and a woman inside.

"I have to go."

"Officer Francis?" he asks.

"Yeah." Even in plain clothes, Francis carries himself like a cop. He stands shoulders back like a soldier, his t-shirt snug around his chest. Most women would swoon at his alpha demeanor—but not me. He's got nothing on my Henry. *My* Henry. I suck in a breath. There's no arguing with my heart.

"Call me later," Sloane says into my ear. "I want to know the plan. Don't commit to anything that's not safe. Promise me."

"I promise. Bye, Sloane." I hang up the phone and slip it into the back pocket of my shorts before waving to Officer Francis and his friend. "Hi, how are you?"

He smiles. "Good. I want you to meet my partner." He gestures to the athletic woman beside him. "This is Officer Swan. She's going to be undercover at the fashion show. Wherever you go, she won't be far behind."

"Nice to finally meet you, Hannah," she says. She glances at Officer Francis. "Shall we get started?"

An hour later, I see the officers out of my apartment and send an email to Sloane with the details of what's going down on the day of the 212 fashion show.

On paper, it sounds easy, but Francis warned that it could—and probably will—go off script fairly quickly. Davis is unpredictable.

***

The morning of July first, I wake to a gut full of knots and lie in bed, convincing myself that today will go as planned. Sloane assured me that even if it doesn't, he can deal. He's got

Gerald and his crew of lawyers and a good PR team to reframe the story. Without evidence of Sloane going anywhere with Candy and Crystal, the video is nothing more than proof of a good deed. A donation to two women to help them get off the street.

The musical ringtone of my cell jolts me upright on the bed. It's Davis.

Swinging my legs over the edge of the mattress, I clear my throat and tap the button to accept his call. "Hello?"

"You ready, Hannah Banana?"

"I've never been more ready," I lie. "Would you believe Sloane had the nerve to email me an invite to the after-party?" I scoff. "Fucking bastard."

He laughs a creepy cackle-like sound. "I might have to take that off your hands so I can watch the fallout of Sloane's demise firsthand."

"It's all yours. I'll print it out and bring it with me today." Grabbing my notebook from my nightstand, I glance at the questions Officer Francis gave me to ask. "Did you decide on a place to meet today? And a time? The fashion show starts at two, but I imagine it'll be pretty busy by one o'clock."

He hums. "What time will the doors open to let people in?"

"As far as I know, they won't let anyone but staff in before twelve-thirty. At least that was the plan a few weeks ago," I add, trying to sound a little unsure.

"Fine. Let's plan for one. I have an important job for you today. I hope you're up for it."

My stomach lurches, but I try to remain calm and keep my voice even. I didn't spend the last two weeks trying to win Davis over for nothing. "What's that?"

"I was at the Plaza last night. They've set up giant screens on either side of the runway."

"Okay…" I swallow the saliva building in the back of my throat. I know exactly which screens he's talking about. They're massive.

Davis laughs again, the same nasally chuckle he gets when he's growing excited. "I'm going to do more than just release the video to the press. I'm going to take over the screens and show New York the scumbag that is *Henry Sloane*."

"Oh my god." I should have known. He wants to humiliate Sloane in front of everyone. I shake off my surprise before he thinks I'm against his idea. "You're a genius. How can I help?"

I can practically hear Davis smiling in my ear. "I need you to find out which computer is connected to the screens, and I want you to distract whoever's running it. I'll do the rest."

My stomach sinks. The video we made is slated to play on a loop. There may not be *anyone* running it. "I can do that. With a little luck, maybe it'll be someone I know."

"That's what I'm hoping."

"How will I know where to find you?"

My question is met with eerie silence.

"Davis? You there?"

"I'm here. I'm thinking. Take your phone. I'll text you around one o'clock."

"Okay, that works." Ugh. It's a good thing I'm not a cop. I'm too agreeable.

Ending the call with Davis, I flop back on the bed. "Why me?" I groan.

My bedroom door bursts open as Vi barges into my room, and I bolt upright again. "Jesus. What the hell?"

"I'm sorry I didn't knock, I know you hate that," she slurs in one long rambled breath. "But guess what just came for you?"

"Oh god, now what?" If it's another gadget, I'm going to lose it.

She glances toward my bedroom door, and I follow the direction of her gaze.

"We're ready!" she calls.

Tessa glides through the doorway like a dancer, twirling around with a beautiful teal dress held out in front of her. "Ta-da!"

Vi squees at a volume too loud for nine in the morning, and I scrunch up my face. "Ow, Vi. Knock it off. Jesus." My interest piqued, I climb off the bed and take the dress from Tessa. My heart stumbles over itself as Sloane's name slips from my mouth on a whisper. Gorgeous is an understatement.

"There's also a note." Tessa passes me an envelope that's no bigger than a business card. "We didn't read it."

Laying the dress on my bed, I sit down before my wobbly legs give out and remove the card.

Neither blue as the darkest ocean, nor cerulean as the summer sky.

Only teal for Hannah.

~ S.

"Aww." I press the card against my chest and swoon. So sweet.

Forcing myself to get up and moving, I shoo the girls from my room and head for the shower. Once my hair is dry, Vi demands I let her pin it up in some kind of fancy twist while Tessa does my makeup. "This is overkill, guys. It's going to look like I'm trying too hard."

"It's a fashion show, Hannah! *Everyone* is going to be dolled up to the max—even us!" Violet claps with obvious delight. "I'm so excited!"

"She's right. Plus, you want to knock Sloane's socks off," Tessa adds.

"You mean his pants," Vi quips.

The three of us laugh, but it soon grows quiet in the room. Vi sets her hand on my shoulder. "Be careful today."

Aw, sweet Vi. "I will. I know you'll both be rooting for me from afar."

Tessa nods. "We'll find you after the show."

"Are you sure we can't just come with you?" Vi asks. "Is it that big a deal if we arrive together? We could be your bodyguards."

I shake my head. "Davis said to come alone. I don't want to do anything that might spook him."

"Hannah's right, honey. This is one instance where we shouldn't meddle. And by *we*, I mean *you*." Tessa kisses Vi gently on the lips to soften the blow of her words. "Let the police do their job. We'll see Hannah after the show."

She nods. "Okay. We'd better hurry up."

In my tiny bedroom, Vi and Tessa help me into my dress so I don't mess up my hair.

Tessa zips me up before whistling a cat-call. "Sloane's on point, Hannah. You look hella good in teal."

I stare at my reflection, lost for words. Sloane knows how to pick a dress, I'll give him that. It's stunning. A simple, classic cut that hugs my curves and accentuates my waist. It's perfectly me.

My eyes find Vi and Tessa's in the mirror as my revelation

come out in a whisper. "I love him so much."

"Aww." Vi's hand slips into Tessa's. "We know. It's pretty clear he loves you, too."

I smile at the recollection of all the little ways he's shown it this week. Even with access to all that money, he chose inexpensive ways to show he cares. Hazelnut coffee delivered every morning. Text messages throughout the day to see how it's going. The selfie he took of him eating yogurt from a mug.

I wring my fingers, my eyes still locked on my reflection. "I'm really nervous, guys. What if I fuck this up? What if the whole plan goes to hell?"

Tessa grips my shoulder. "You've got this, Hannah. You've made too many spreadsheets for this plan to be anything but flawless."

The corner of my mouth twitches into an almost smile. "That's true." We spent last night role-playing every possible way today could play out. I'm as prepared as I can be under the circumstances.

**

The forty dollar cab ride to the Plaza Hotel is well worth the money. It keeps me cool and gives me time to calm my nerves. But as nervous as I am, excitement also courses through me. Today I get to see all my hard work, my designs and my plans come to fruition. And today I get to see Sloane.

The taxi stops at the curbside in front of the Plaza, and I hand the driver some money over the back of the seat, thanking him quickly before stepping out into the muggy July air.

The crowd is buzzing with excitement, women decked out in designer dresses and men looking slick in tailored suits. I make a mental note to thank Vi and Tessa for dolling me up. I fit right in with the Manhattan Elite.

After checking my phone for the millionth time, I slip it back inside the tiny clutch hooked over my shoulder. I'm early. A good ten minutes before Davis is expecting me.

Making my way through the masses, I head for the Grand Ballroom, stopping mid-step as I enter the mighty space. Opulence and luxury all but take my breath away. It's unbelievable. Jutting out from the elegant stage at the far end of the room, the gleaming catwalk extends toward me. White linen curtains billow softly, creating an air of mystery as to what's happening behind the scenes.

A technician steps out from behind the curtain and fiddles with the microphone on the podium that's positioned off to the side of the catwalk.

My gaze flicks toward the parted fabric, to the lone dark suit standing tall in a sea of feminine clothes.

Sloane.

He meets my eyes, nothing more than a subtle nod of his head to let me know he sees me. *He's not taking any chances.*

And neither should I.

I force myself to look away, instead, admiring the massive posters displayed around the ballroom. The designs haven't changed much from my mockups. My insides swell with pride. They look amazing.

#ThisIsMe

The hashtag flickers across the massive screens that flank either side of the stage, and my stomach launches itself into my throat. Those are the screens Davis wants to hijack, but I can't let that happen.

I won't.

I scan the growing crowd for anyone suspicious, but it's no use. Davis could be anywhere.

A familiar-looking woman catches my eye about ten feet away. It takes me a moment to clue in who she is before I quickly look the other way.

Officer Swan.

I almost forgot. My shoulders relax a tiny bit. I'm not alone in this. NYPD is in the crowd, several plainclothes officers dressed up to blend in with the masses. I've got eyes and ears all over me this afternoon. I'm safe.

But is Sloane?

Vibrations against my hip tear me from my thoughts. I pull out my phone and skim the incoming messages from Davis.

I'm here.

Head to the south end of the building and wait for me.

I'll find you.

I shoot off a quick *okay* and slip my phone back inside my clutch.

With one last glance toward the stage, I straighten my necklace and blow out a puff of air. Davis may have a plan, but ours is better.

It's showtime.

CHAPTER seventeen

Creeping past a sign that says *Employee Access Only*, I head toward the south end of the Plaza—at least that's where I think I'm headed. Geography is not my forte. And short of pulling out my phone to look at the compass app, I'll have to take my chances.

This side of the building is all but dead, except for the handful of hotel staff scurrying about on a clear-cut mission. They pass me without blinking. It's not their job to watch for interlopers, and for that, I'm grateful.

A security guard rounds the corner, heading in my direction. In a panic, I duck into the first room I come to and pray there's no one inside. The door closes behind me with a solid click, and I scan the space.

The Press Room. Phew.

Rows of chairs have been arranged at one end of the room,

and a table and podium have been set up at the other. Behind the podium, a large poster board plastered with #ThisIsMe is positioned as the backdrop for when Henry is speaking to the press.

"Hello, Hannah Banana."

The utterance of my name rips me from my thoughts, and I whip around to face the door. My body tenses. A short, stocky man in a black suit stands just inside the doorway. He grins at me, and recognition hits me in the gut like a bag of cement. His front tooth is missing the glob of chocolate, but I would recognize him anywhere. It's the man from the event I helped Candace cater. His suit is less purple than the Austin Powers one he wore that night, though this one is still much too large for him. It hangs off him like the boxy cuts men wore in the eighties.

"Davis?"

He steps toward me, and I take a quick sweep of the room to see what other options I have to escape, just in case. An emergency exit. Good.

"I wasn't sure if you would recognize me," he says. "I'm flattered that you do."

My toes curl in disgust. It's only because he reminds me of Danny Devito in the nineties—the glasses, the bald spot, the shit-eating grin.

He openly ogles me, peeling my dress away with his eyes, and I try not to shiver. His creep factor is off the charts. "You look stunning in that color," he says, licking his lips.

I swallow the bile rising in my throat. Blech. "Thank you." The word comes out more nervous than I'd hoped, and I force myself to smile back. "You look nice, too." I inwardly cringe at the phony compliment. There's a good reason I got a C in high school drama. I'm a terrible liar.

A deep V forms on his brow. "Don't bullshit, Hannah. There are only so many places a man of my stature can shop."

Shit. I've unintentionally poked his sore spot.

"You know, women bitch about how hard it is to buy clothes. Well, *boohoo.*" Davis smacks his palm against his chest. "What about us men? Not all of us have bodies like Henry Sloane."

"I understand," I say, trying my best to sound sympathetic.

"No. You have no idea. Women already corner the fucking market. Seventy-one percent of stores are for you, and you're still not happy. But, me? The bulk of my measly twenty-nine percent is for hot, young studs or grandpas," he bursts. "That leaves me with bullshit big and tall stores. And in case you haven't noticed, I'm not exactly tall!"

Understanding dawns on me and my nerves settle just a tad. "Sloane's on Fifth doesn't carry clothes that fit you."

"Neither do any of the other bullshit stores on that street. I don't even bother anymore."

"What about having your clothes tailored?" My phone buzzes against my hip, but I ignore it, hoping Davis doesn't become suspicious of the noises coming from my purse.

His face grows red. "That defeats the fucking purpose! If I have the money, I should be able to wear the label!"

I get it. Of all the people, he could complain to, I can understand his plight. But there's no need to be a psycho. I throw my palms up between us when Davis strides closer. "Have you considered lobbying the designers? Or talking to them?"

Davis reaches into the breast pocket of his suit, and my heart rate skyrockets. What if he pulls a gun? I step back and prepare myself to leap out of the way.

To my relief, it's just a cell phone and a small black USB stick. He waves them in front of me. "*This* is how I lobby. And what a better place to bring Sloane to his knees than here."

"But he's changed," I blurt. "He listened and made a whole new line of clothes with bigger sizes. Maybe he'll do that for his men's line too?"

Davis's eyes round to saucers. "I fucking knew it!" His grip tightens around his phone. "You're on his side." He looks around, paranoid. "Aren't you?"

I shake my head. "No. Never."

"I don't believe you." He taps on his phone and turns away from me.

"What are you doing?" I move to see around him, but he keeps turning his back to me. "Davis, wait."

Peeking over his shoulder, I catch sight of what looks like a video thumbnail, and I panic. I grab his arm and reach around to slap at his phone. My palm connects with the screen, and it clatters to the ground.

Davis stoops to pick it up, but my reflexes are faster. With the flick of my foot, I kick it across the floor and watch it slide beneath the rows of chairs like a hockey puck into a net. "Hah!" Final score: Hannah 1, Davis 0.

"You *bitch*." Davis lunges at me with a speed that defies his stature, and we collapse to the floor, him on top of me. I shriek, more out of surprise than fear, but it's cut off by the pressure of his hands around my neck.

Thrashing underneath him, I claw at his fingers, digging my

nails into his flesh. He's crazy. His dark brown eyes are black with fury, his nostrils flared as he grunts a slur of nonsense about the injustice of his circumstance.

My hip grinds itself into the floor under Davis's weight, and pain shoots up my side just as the door bursts open.

Thank God.

"Hannah!" Sloane's booming voice echoes in the room followed by Officer Swan's angry shouts for Davis to raise his hands.

Taking advantage of the sudden distraction, I jerk on Davis's fingers, peeling them back until there's an audible pop. His high-pitched wail hurts my ears, but his grip on my throat disappears, along with his body as Davis is ripped off of me.

I cough and sputter as I catch my breath and watch as Sloane slams Davis face down into the floor like a rag doll. His forehead connects with the tile with a thud, and Officer Swan jumps on top of his paunchy body. Even in a cocktail dress, that woman is impressive. She twists Davis's arms behind him, her knee digging into his back as she cuffs him and reads him his rights.

Relief floods my system like a blocked dam that's given way, and I blink away the oncoming tears. It's over.

Sloane drops to his knees beside me and pulls me into his lap. His eyes are wide with concern as his fingers trace my neck. "Are you all right? Oh, god, Hannah."

"It's okay. I'm not hurt." I try to take his hand, but he raises mine to his lips.

He kisses my fingers. "Your neck is red. Oh my god, he was choking you."

"I'm good. Honestly." I clear the raspiness from my throat

and point toward where Davis's phone slid beneath the chairs. "His phone. Down there."

Sloane nods. "Don't worry about any of that. The police will get it."

As if summoned by Sloane's words, several tuxedo-clad officers enter the room and speak quietly with Officer Swan. She turns to us. "We'll take him out the side entrance to avoid any more attention."

"Thank you." Sloane peers at me. "Are you okay to get up?"

He hooks one arm under my legs once I nod, and he pushes himself off the floor with my body still cocooned in his arms. He sets me in a chair. "I want someone to look you over."

"No." I shake my head vehemently. "I'm fine. And look—" I point to the analog clock on the wall "—it's almost time." Standing from the chair, I brush off my dress. Other than a sore hip, I really am okay. All things considered, it's hard to tell I've even been in a scuffle—at least from what I can see.

Sloane's lips press together, unconvinced.

"You can check me over later if you're concerned," I tell him, smiling sweetly.

His eyebrow ticks upward, and I waggle mine.

He grins, his earlier concern waning. "You're amazing, Hannah. And crazy. I should have stood my ground and kept you out of this ploy. It almost backfired."

"But it didn't. And he wasn't able to send the video."

"Sorry to interrupt." Officer Francis appears at Sloane's side. "Ms. O'Keefe, we need to get your statement."

"Would it be all right if I watch the show and give my statement after?" I turn to Henry. "Please. I don't want to miss it."

"I think that's fair." Sloane glances at Officer Francis. "Don't you?"

"I suppose." Officer Francis must have gotten Cs in drama too because he's clearly not happy with that option.

"Good." Sloane doesn't give Francis the chance to amend his words. He takes my hand. "Let's not keep them waiting."

***

From my front-row seat, I watch model after model walk the catwalk, each one dressed in an outfit that suits her unique shape. The entire show is flawless, and by the end, when all of the women take the stage and say a synchronized *This Is Me*, I'm close to tears. Sloane appears from behind the curtains, and the crowd erupts as he moves toward the podium. He addresses the audience, thanking his designers, his staff, and most of all, his customers for their support.

"And we wouldn't be here today if it weren't for one other important person in my life. Hannah—" He curls his finger in my direction. "Can you come up here and join me, please?"

Oh shit. My mouth falls open as I glance around the room. There's no escaping; everyone is peering in my direction.

Beside me, Pam tugs my arm, grinning. "Go on."

Focusing on putting one foot in front of the other, I make my way to Sloane, silently plotting all the ways I'm going to get him back for this.

Once I reach him, he grins at me before speaking into the mic. "Everyone, I'd like to introduce you to Hannah O'Keefe. Everything you see here today—" he gestures to the models, and to the posters around the room "—Hannah had some part in making. She is a huge supporter of inclusivity, both in clothing and in people in general. And that's why she is now the official brand manager for Sloane's clothing, including the 212 portfolio."

My head whips around to face Sloane. "What are you doing?"

He grins, leaning away from the mic to whisper in my ear. "Giving you the position you deserve. I want you working right beside me, Hannah. Not with Hudson Roth, not with anyone but me." Back in front of the microphone, he adds, "If you have ideas on what else you want to see moving forward, let Hannah know. Add hashtag ThisIsMe to your posts and Hannah will see them. I trust her to take your ideas and run with them. Thank you."

The crowd breaks into another round of applause and Sloane points to the microphone, inviting me to say something. Way to put me on the spot. Jesus.

Standing on my toes, I adjust the microphone so it points toward my mouth. "Thank you, Henry." I glance at Sloane before facing the audience. In the distance, Vi and Tessa wave at me and scream. I shoot them a smile. "I think most of us here in this room today have experienced the pain of trying on clothes and having none of them fit—myself included. I won't lie. It sucks. The goal of the 212 pilot is to provide a clothing line that is fashionable and classy while taking into consideration the variety of shapes and sizes that women come in. Whether you're an apple, pear or an hourglass like me, we hope you'll find a key piece of clothing to add to your wardrobe. Don't camouflage your curves with too-big clothes. Visit Sloane's on Fifth and proudly tell the world, *This is Me*."

The roar that fills the Plaza ballroom deafens my ears. I smile at Sloane, and he leans in close. "I love you, Hannah."

Pulling back, I grin at him. "I love you, too, *Mr. Sloane.*"

Without warning, his mouth closes over mine, and the crowd grows impossibly louder. My heart thumps against my chest.

After a few soft kisses, Sloane hugs me to his chest, his head nuzzled in the crook of my neck. "HR is going to kill me."

"Do you care?"

His laugh rumbles against my skin. "Not one bit. I'll tell Sandra that I couldn't help it. After all, *this is me.*"

***

Three months after the successful launch of 212, Henry and I are back at Bastien's studio, but this time it's Sloane's turn on the pedestal.

"I'm too old to be modeling," he grumbles.

"You are not. You're barely thirty." I stand off to one side, where Sloane once watched me get measured. In just a tight, black pair of boxer briefs, the studio light emphasizes every chiseled ab. If I had a body like his, I'd parade around the streets every chance I got. "You're the reason the men's line sells so well. Embrace it."

He scoffs. "I don't remember it being this bright." He swipes the back of his arm across his forehead. "Was it always this bright in here?"

"Mmm-hmm," Bastien hums. "Now, for God's sake, keep still."

"I'm trying. Hannah, remind me why I'm doing this again?"

I laugh. "Because you gave me carte blanche."

"On the expansion of the 212 product line."

"Yeah, but this a crossover. A his and hers collection. Still counts. Everyone will love it. I have a name picked out and everything."

He grumbles something about taking liberties before adding, "You're enjoying this way too much."

I shrug. "Payback's a bitch, Mr. Sloane. Before you give somebody carte blanche, you ought to think of the consequences."

A smile tugs at the corner of his mouth. "I'm starting to rethink this whole engagement, Bastien. I'm a little worried Hannah's going to turn into one of those crazy bridezillas. What do you think? Run while I still can?"

I glance down at the intricate diamond ring on my finger and smile. "Feel free to poke him, Bastien."

Sloane's eyes grow wide. "Bastien knows better than to— Ouch! You bastard!"

"Whoops. Sorry."

I bark a laugh at Bastien's unconvincing apology. He grins at me, and I give him a thumbs-up before blowing a kiss to Sloane.

Sloane reaches down to rub his thigh. "You're kissing that better later," he warns.

I waggle my eyebrows, recalling our impromptu tryst in the change room not thirty minutes ago.

"At *home,*" Bastien bursts. "Pour l'amour de Dieu. For the love of God, *not in my changing room!*"

Sloane's eyes meet mine in the mirror as heat rushes to my face.

Busted.

Loved the book?
Consider leaving a review.

Thank you for purchasing Losing Manhattan, and most of all, thank you for reading it! 🤍

If you enjoyed the story, please consider leaving a review on Amazon, Goodreads or Bookbub to help others gauge whether Losing Manhattan belongs on their bookshelf.

Thank you!

Also by Peyton James

Naked in New York Series
Billionaire contemporary romance - read in any order.
Losing Manhattan
Dating Brooklyn
Playing Chelsea (Fall 2022)

Chasing Lucy
An enemies-to-lovers contemporary romance.

Dating Brooklyn
(A Naked in New York Novel, #2)

When it comes to love, there are only two types of people in this world: those who believe it exists and the rest of us—the realists. All that lovey-dovey crap you feel sometimes … it's in your head. That's right. Hormones.

For the past five years, I've been dishing out dating advice to anyone who'll listen. But if you write to Ask Adelaide expecting syrupy words or fairytale musings, you'll be sorely disappointed. I prefer to slap you with a dose of cold, hard truth, minus the sugar. You can thank me later.

Not to be a hypocrite, of course, I follow all the rules I preach: No second dates, no sleepovers, no exceptions. One red flag and I will ding-dong ditch you faster than you can blink.

No one has better control of their heart than me.

Or so I thought …

Until Nash Evans strolls into my life all strong but silent and gorgeous as sin. The last thing I expect is for him to turn my world on end and threaten to evict me.

It turns out Nash has rules of his own, and since he's my new landlord, I need to comply.

Except I can't.

Background checks are not my friend. And if Nash does a little digging, he'll discover I didn't exist beyond five years ago. Or worse, he'll uncover all the secrets I've been trying to outrun.

All books in the Naked in New York Series can be read in any order. Happily ever after, guaranteed.

Chapter One

On any given day, there are six million singles searching for love in New York City. Some will go it alone, swiping left or right, relying on fate to meet their perfect match. Some will turn to friends for advice, and others will settle for meaningless hookups.

The rest will turn to me.

Adelaide Quinn, New York's toughest online dating coach. I'm tough because I've lived through love. I've lived through the highest highs and the cruelest lows. I've had my walls torn down and my heart demolished. I've been hurt, lied to, cheated on and misled.

But I'm good now. Because now, I can see through the bullshit. It's my superpower—and it's how I earn my living. I teach people to spot the fake and the phony. To settle for nothing but the best. And more importantly, I teach them when and how to walk away.

There's no denying I've broken up more relationships than I've rescued. But I've also saved many from inevitable heartbreak. Love me or hate me, this is who I am. I speak the truth. Take my advice or leave it. It's up to you.

***

Dump him.

Ditch her.

Walk away.

There are hundreds of ways to say it. Sure, I could find fluffier words, but sometimes people need a dose of cold, hard truth, minus the sugar.

My haters call me Doctor Doom. I get it. I'm not exactly forthcoming in the hope department. But my lovers—and there are plenty—swear by my advice.

I'm not a doctor. Technically, I'm not even a dating coach, not in the traditional sense. I don't have a specialized degree in anything but tried-and-true experience in what not to do. People ask for my advice, and I dish it. The end.

Dear Adelaide,

I attract bad boys. You know the kind: torn jeans, tats, questionable morals. They ALWAYS break my heart. It's been months since I went out on a date because I don't trust myself to avoid the naughty ones. Where are all the nice guys? Please help.

Sincerely,

Nervous To Date Again

Dear Nervous,

You have good reason to be hesitant. There are lots of jerks out there! I've been on A TON of dates, and let me tell you, it's not the tats that make them naughty. There are plenty of clean-cut guys who are just as duplicitous.

But regardless of how someone looks, don't waste your time trying to change anyone you date. If they have a trait that goes against your values, cut your losses and move on. The next guy you date could also be a dud, or he might be your Prince Charming. You won't know unless you try.

Yours,

Adelaide

Prince Charming? A quiet scoff escapes my mouth as I click the button to post my lame reply on social media. Like it or not, I'm taking Anja's advice. She's the PR pro, not me, and I hired her for a reason. Of course, that doesn't stop me from wondering how much of her guidance is by the book and how much is from her heart. Unlike me, she's a sucker for the lovey-dovey crap. She's always on my case to give readers a little more hope in my answers, even if it's only a sliver.

I snap my laptop shut.

If it were only up to me, I'd have told Nervous not to get their hopes up. Dating in New York is like the world's cruelest game show. It takes strategy, skill, and a helluva lot of luck. And even if you follow all the rules and ace every damn challenge, you might never walk away with the prize.

It's certainly not a competition *I'm* looking to win. One day, I might find myself married with two-point-five children and a weekend home in the Hamptons. But I'm also a realist. It's probably not in the cards for me, and I'm okay with that. Perfectly okay.

A musical ringtone cuts through the silence of Angelo's Restaurant, and I snatch up my phone from its spot on the checkered tablecloth before it can disturb the other customers. Not that it matters. Angelo's is almost always empty until the dinner rush, and even then, it's never filled near capacity.

Anja's picture lights up the screen, and I tap the button to answer without bothering to say hello. "If this is about what I wrote to the guy wanting advice about the curve in his penis, the answer is no. I don't care if my response was blunt. Dick pics are a hard no for me."

Holding the phone away from my ear while Anja giggles, I glance around the restaurant. Rosa smiles at me from behind the front counter, and I give her a wave. She points toward the kitchen, then holds up two fingers. My lunch is nearly ready. Thank God, because I'm starving.

"I don't care about that right now," Anja says, still laughing. "I have *amazing* news. And it's penis-free, I promise. I need you here, like ASAP."

I fight the urge to groan. She may be my friend and the brains behind *Ask Adelaide*, but Anja's idea of amazing news always means more work for me. As it is, I barely have time to sleep. "I would if I could, but I've got Angelo's lasagna coming my way, and you know I won't let that go cold for anything— not even the most *amazing* news."

"All right, fine," she grumbles. "I can't believe you're making me sit on this."

I almost feel bad for making her wait, but I already made the trek to Manhattan once this week for a mid-year check-in with her team. I owe a lot of my success to her. She took my little blog about dating misadventures and helped me turn it into a lucrative business.

"You can tell me now," I suggest, "if it's that important." She won't. She never shares details like this over the phone; it's too easy for me to say no.

"This is too huge for that, Addie." She pauses as if she's hoping I'll change my mind. "Fine. Can you come tomorrow? It'll be worth the trip, I promise."

"It better be. And nothing too early." Commuting to Manhattan is terrible at the best of times, but the morning is the worst.

"Great. Nine?"

I laugh under my breath. "Got anything later?"

She huffs in my ear, and I catch the distinct sound of her shuffling papers around on her disaster of a desk. To call her disorganized would be a compliment. She's a slob with a capital S. But she's also a genius when it comes to PR and marketing. I've already decided to renew our contract in the fall. Anja and her team at Skyward Digital really know their stuff. "Okay, fine," she says. "Eleven. That's the best I can do. Work with me, please."

"That's better. You know it takes forever to get to the 2-1-2 from Brooklyn."

"It takes forever to get *anywhere* from where you live."

"That's not true." And if it was, so what? Everything I need and love is here in Brooklyn. Cobble Hill has it all. It's like a tiny village inside a city.

"Seriously, Addie. I can hook you up with a realtor. It's time to invest that hard-earned money and move. Manhattan is where it's at."

My insides twist into instant knots. It's been five years since I moved into the studio apartment above Angelo's Restaurant, and though it leaves a lot to be desired, there are lots of plusses, too. Fresh, authentic garlic loaf whenever my heart desires. Rosa's mouth-watering lasagna. That spicy arrabbiata sauce they drizzle over the pasta. The plusses mostly revolve around food, but it's more than that. Papa Angelo and Rosa are like family. They're also my landlords, and if they lose my rent, they'll be struggling more than they already are. They gave me a job, took me in when I'd lost everything. I won't turn my back on them now.

"I'll think about it," I lie. "When it's time to move, you'll be my first call."

"Good. And I swear Hudson is the best. He sells real estate before it's even on the market. *And*, he's very easy on the eyes, if you know what I mean."

While Anja goes on and on about her hot realtor friend, I sip on my water and um-hmm in all the right places. She's always got a man within her sights.

The smooth, low timbre of a familiar voice has my eyes snapping to the front of the restaurant. "No thank you, Rosa. I've already eaten."

He's back! The Suit. Only he's not in a suit today, just slacks and a dress shirt, no tie. He pats his stomach, waving away the plate Rosa is offering. "I really can't."

"Hello? Earth to Adelaide," Anja sing-songs. "You there?"

"I'm here. I need to let you go. My food is going to be here in a sec."

Ending the call, I set my phone back on the table beside my laptop. I want to get closer to The Suit. This is the second time this week he's popped by and disappeared into Papa Angelo's office. He looks like a lawyer. Or a banker. Definitely a Manhattanite. But he could also be one of those nasty developers scouring the town. As it is, three of the properties on this block have been snatched up. Rumors are swirling about tearing the whole strip down and replacing it with some cookie-cutter monstrosity. Soon, they'll call us *Condo Capital* instead of Cobble Hill.

Regardless, Rosa and Papa Angelo aren't sellouts. I've seen firsthand how quickly Papa scuttles those developers out before they can even sniff the potential profits. Angelo's has history. It's rich with authentic Italian culture. Hell, Angelo's has been in business since Papa was a little boy, and his own Papi ran the place. He wouldn't give this up, no matter how hard-pressed he is for money.

"Lunchtime, *cara mia*." Rosa's sweet voice calls out to me, and I stand from where I've been tucked away in the corner booth.

She makes her way around the counter with my plate, but I hurry toward her. "I'll come get it, Rosa, thank you." For sixty-eight, she's in fabulous shape and could be across the room to me in moments, but I have other motives for wanting to get my food.

Next to Rosa, Papa speaks with The Suit. The men are deep in conversation, something about wine and pasta and secret ingredients you can only find in Italy. That's got to be it! This guy wants Rosa's recipes. But why? To sell them off to the highest bidder? To claim them as his own?

Papa waves me over before Rosa can pass me my plate. "*Ciao, Bella.* Come. This is Signor Evans." He turns to the businessman. "Mr. Evans, Addie."

The Suit holds out his hand, and I don't hesitate to shake it. You can tell a lot about a man from his handshake, and surprisingly, The Suit gets a pass. His grip is firm but not overbearing. It's what I describe to my readers as the *I'm your equal* handshake. At first glance, The Suit checks out, but I'm not done yet. I won't let Rosa and Papa fall prey to a hustler. They deserve a fair price if they're going to sell the recipes they took years to perfect.

Raking the man over, I search for hints of deceit: wayward eyes, fidgeting, any obvious signs of ill intent.

Nothing.

Dammit. I'm off my game today. Worse, it might be that pretty face throwing me off. The light dusting of scruff that coats his jawline, all perfectly trimmed and angled to draw the eye toward velvet-soft lips.

"Please, call me Nash."

"Nash." I try out his name on my tongue. It's different. Unassuming. Not at all what I'd expected. Even his eyes are friendly. So wide and wonderfully expressive that soon I'm lost in their deep brown depths. Hypnotized by swirls of caramel.

"Pleasure to meet you, Addie."

I blink away his spell and drop his hand. "And you."

Nash gestures in the direction of my booth. "You were here the last time I came in. Same spot. You must be one of the regulars Mr. Angelo mentioned."

My traitorous head nods before I can stop it, and my mouth goes rogue as well, adding, "I come here to write. The amazing food is a bonus." I glance from Papa and Rosa to my lasagna. It's getting cold, but for some odd reason, I don't mind.

His eyebrow quirks and I follow the movement to his dark brown hair. It's neat and trimmed along the sides, but the top is longer and leans toward unruly.

"That's interesting," he says, drawing my eyes back to his lips. "What do you write?"

I shake my head. "It's hardly worth mentioning."

"Can you give me a hint?" Nash smiles at me, and my heartbeat stutters at the tiny imperfection that appears on his cheek. A dimple. One side only, and it adds to his appeal.

Playfulness bubbles through me. I had him pegged as a stuck-up suit, but he's beginning to prove me wrong. "Nope. It's highly classified. If I told you, I'd have to kill you."

He chuckles as my mouth clamps shut, and I inwardly kick myself for my reckless slip. I shouldn't be hinting that there's anything to hide. That will only invite more probing.

Only a handful of people know I'm the infamous Doctor Doom. And while I only receive a few empty threats each month, I don't relish the idea of my haters knowing my face in the flesh.

And worse, if anyone did some real digging, they'd discover that Adelaide Quinn didn't exist beyond five years ago.

Not even Papa Angelo and Rosa know my story. It's nobody's business. Not my birth name, my past, my criminal record.

Papa Angelo pats my shoulder. "Addie is the upstairs tenant."

Nash looks my way, and his eyebrows shoot up toward his hairline before settling. "Oh, I didn't realize."

Warning bells ring inside my head. "Realize *what*?"

Rosa peers at her husband, frowning.

Red flag.

"Addie, we—" Rosa pauses, glancing at the men as if she's unsure if she's allowed to continue.

"It's okay." Nash tucks his hand into his pocket and pulls out a business card before handing it to me. "We've finished the paperwork. It's official."

Red flag.

My thumb smooths over the ultra-glossy finish. Nash Evans. Investa Property Development, Inc.

No. My insides sour as my gaze rolls slowly up to meet Nash's inquisitive stare. I should have known. The fancy clothes. The smooth talk and witty banter. He's a goddamn developer.

"Oh shit." My words come out in a whisper. "You bought Angelo's."

Nash peers around the empty restaurant before looking back at me. "The building, actually."

Red flag. Red flag. Red flag.

"The building?"

"Yes." His eyebrow ticks upward. "I guess that makes me your landlord."

Dating Brooklyn will be available on Amazon on January 5, 2022.

Connect with Peyton James

Please don't hesitate to reach out to me for information about upcoming releases or to share your feedback on my work. I love hearing stories and ideas from my readers. Want to see a spin-off starring another character? Let me know. It might already be in the works!

Website: www.authorpeytonjames.com
Facebook: @AuthorPeytonJames
Twitter: @AuthorPeytonJ
Instagram: @AuthorPeytonJames
TikTok: @AuthorPeytonJames

Join my official mailing list.

Join the official Peyton James mailing list to receive occasional newsletters with details on upcoming releases, giveaways, offers, and sneak peeks.

Subscribers are the first to receive information on release dates, so if you want to be among the first to receive news on upcoming releases, join today at www.authorpeytonjames.com.

About the Author

Peyton James writes contemporary romance stories about love and loss and everything in between. She is the author of the Naked in New York series, as well as several standalone novels, including Chasing Lucy. By day, Peyton is a Communications Specialist for one of the fastest-growing municipalities in Canada. In her spare time, you can find her in the sunshine with her four children or stealthily hidden from the chaos writing on her MacBook.

Made in United States
North Haven, CT
07 July 2022

21039790R00129